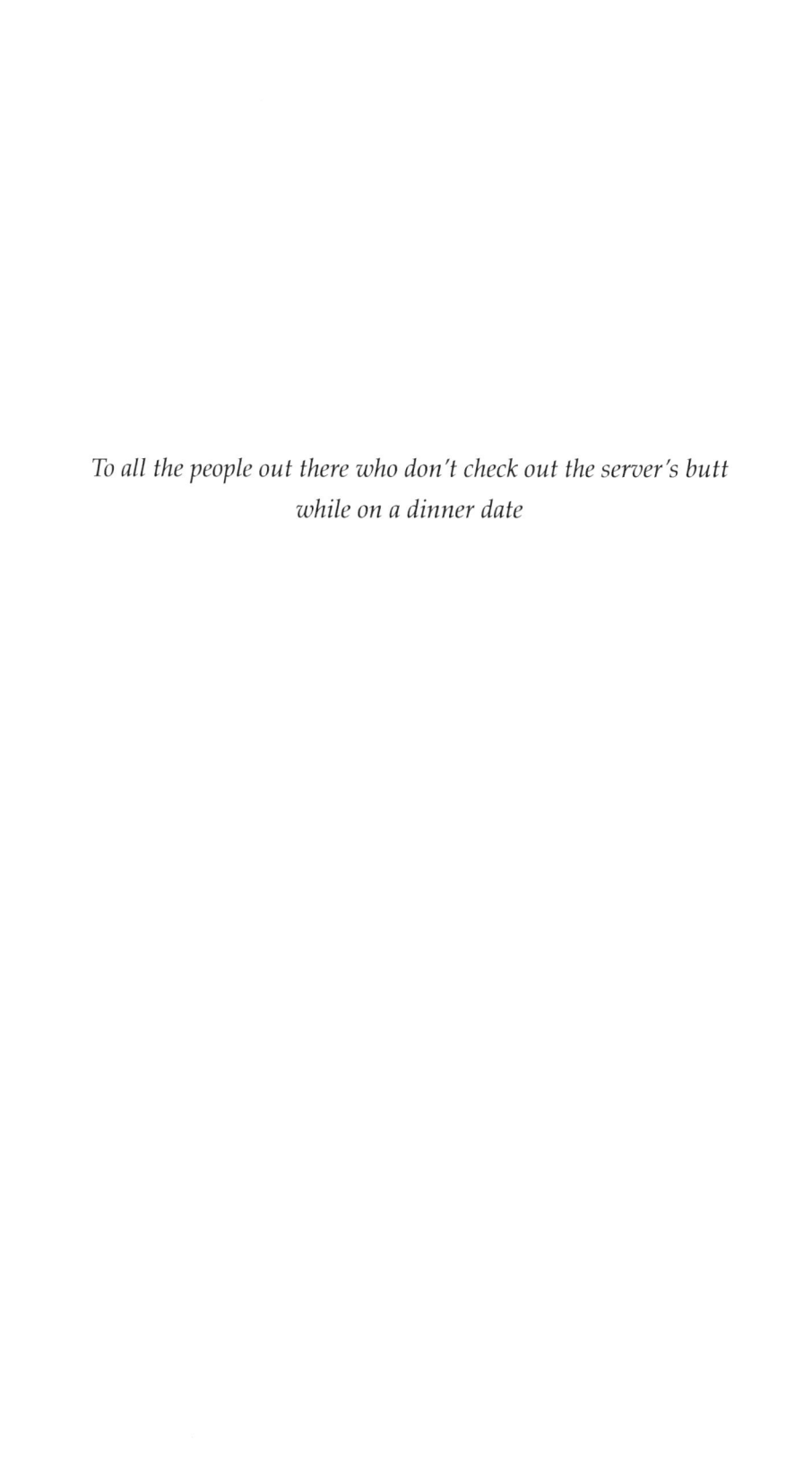

To all the people out there who don't check out the server's butt while on a dinner date

NOVEL DESCRIPTION

He's a prince longing for freedom.
She's a baker yearning for the ultimate love story.
Together, they'll discover that sometimes the
sweetest magic lies in unexpected places.

Rosalyn's enchanted scones bring magic to every bite at The Sconery and Teashop. With a glitter-sneezing caticorn and a thriving business, all Rosalyn needs is a romance as sweet as her baking. When a mysterious Rune elf strides into Moonshine Hollow, bringing secrets and devastating charm, her perfectly-measured life crumbles faster than a day-old scone.

Bjorn is no ordinary elf. A secret prince looking for an escape, he's determined to forge his own path far from the expectations of his royal family. When he's tasked with helping a wild unicorn herd suffering from chaotic magic, he's relieved to focus on creatures instead of people. That is, until a certain insistently-friendly baker and her pet crash into his carefully guarded solitude.

As Rosalyn and Bjorn work together to uncover the source of the magical imbalance in horned creatures, sparks fly in more ways than one. Her warmth and charm start to melt his icy walls, but Bjorn's secret could shatter their fragile connection. Rosalyn dreams of the kind of love bards sing about, but will this gruff and guarded prince sweep her off her feet before it's too late?

Must Love Scones and Secrets is a spicy cozy fantasy romance full of enchanted pastries, mischievous caticorns, and a love story that will warm your heart.

What to expect:

- Royal Romance
- Grumpy/Sunshine
- Forced Proximity
- Small-Town Magic
- Animal Companions
- Hidden Identity
- Fish Out of Water
- Found Family
- Guaranteed HEA
- Medium Spice 🌶🌶🌶

Must Love Scones and Secrets is book 1 in the enchanting cozy fantasy *Moonshine Hollow* series, introducing us to the magical town of Moonshine Hollow and its residents. **Each novel in the series can be read as a stand-alone.**

Perfect for lovers of steamy fantasy rom-com, romantasy, and cozy fantasy romance with a dash of spice! Fans of Kimberly Lemming, Heather Fawcett, J Penner, and Cora Crane will devour this super cozy but very passionate tale of magic, romance, and redemption.

Must Love Scones & Secrets

CHAPTER 1
ROSALYN

This had to be the worst first date in history. The orc's loud laugh rippled across The Moonlit Chalice, causing Elder Thornberry's wife, Petunia, to turn from her coveted spot in the garden alcove with a disapproving frown. The elegant restaurant occupied an old merchant's manor. Soft, evening breezes drifted through open glass doors to the wisteria-covered terrace. Fresh roses in crystal vases graced each table, their fragrance mingling with the aroma of bloomberry tarts wafting from the kitchen. I cringed when several diners winced at yet another burst of raucous laughter from my date, their romantic evenings disturbed. The problem wasn't that he was an orc. In fact, orcs were relatively commonplace in Moonshine Hollow. The problem was *him*.

Since tall, muscular, and brooding were my type, I had been more than pleased when Grakkar Steelfist arrived in

Moonshine Hollow. I'd spent days dreaming about how that wall of green muscle would sweep me off my feet, my toes curling in anticipation of passionate nights, believing he would be the love of my life.

The reality was quite different.

The boorish man talked about himself nonstop for at least thirty minutes. He'd just laughed at his own joke before launching into more self-congratulation about his successful trading business. Pushing a lock of red hair over my shoulder, I rested my chin on my hand and considered him as he gobbled down his dish.

"The merchants said they'd never heard a more lucrative idea," he told me. "Huge potential. Enormous. They were so glad I'd come to Moonshine Hollow. No one here has ideas as good as mine."

I highly doubted that.

I opened my mouth to reply, when he continued.

"I shouldn't be surprised, of course. Moonshine Hollow is full of good people, but not killers in business like me. I'll have production flowing and people lining up like ants in a line to buy my goods in no time," he said, then laughed again—loudly.

This time, he earned a shush from Petunia, not that he noticed.

I cringed and mouthed, "I'm sorry," to her and the other refined ladies at her table.

Ugh. I looked back at my date. Was *this* the person I bought a new blue dress for? Was he really the man I'd tried six outfits on to find the perfect, sparkly gown that accented my hair, blue eyes, and glowing blue wings perfectly? My mind wandered to thoughts of life, love, and why I seemed completely cursed when it came to finding a good man.

Was it because I was a pixie? Was it because I was too friendly? Was there something inherently wrong with me that made me choose bad dates over and over again? Or was it that I had decided to ask Grakkar out because I thought he'd be fun for a night—or ten? Maybe that last one had something to do with it, but it had been too long since I'd had a lover, and obviously, I was getting desperate.

I didn't know Grakkar well, but I had been hopeful that I would find the love I had dreamed of somewhere under that shaggy black hair and those piercing amber-colored eyes. My own personal Lord Thornwick—the devilishly handsome, broody, and romantic hero of my favorite novel, *Crown and Crumpets*. Instead, I found a self-absorbed bore.

Grakkar knocked back his drink and set it down on the table with a clunk, wiping his mouth with the back of his hand. "Gods," he said, puffing up his chest, "you should have seen how I handled that trade deal with Master Pepperwort today. That stubborn old gnome thought he could shortchange me on those enchanted crystals. But I showed him who's boss. I told him straight to his face that his pricing was a joke. Everyone in the room was amazed. No one else would dare talk to him like that, but I put him right in his place. I could tell they were all admiring my nerve. No one else dares to talk the way I do."

"Oh?" I murmured, not really giving him an answer. I

actually couldn't remember the last time I'd spoken. Making noises that acknowledged his awesomeness every few moments seemed to satisfy him.

The orc, having finished his dinner, gazed over at my plate. I'd pushed the same carrot back and forth across it for the last twenty minutes, trying to decide whether it would be rude to just leave. After all, I was the one who had invited him to dinner. I couldn't bail, could I?

That said, the fact that he had ordered my dish for me, insisting that he knew the best thing for me to eat, should have been the first red flag. And now, I was left with my plate full of carrots—which I hated—while I was dreaming of bloomberry tarts…and a better dinner companion.

But if not this guy, who? I had almost run out of options in Moonshine Hollow. The dating market had proved no more promising this year than any other. It was beginning to look like I would end up a spinster like my neighbor Winifred Bramblewood. We'd end up gossiping together as we watched all the other couples pass our businesses' windows, Winifred pretending to rearrange her flower bouquets and me standing outside The Sconery and Teashop leaning on a broom while lurking for some new piece of gossip. The idea was so depressing that I wanted to throw myself into Silver River.

Grakkar looked at my plate, then slowly dragged his gaze up my body in a way that should have excited me but made my skin crawl. His eyes lingered on my chest, his gaze bouncing from breast to breast. I started to wonder if he'd forgotten I had a face. When he finally met my eyes, his expression was hungry in a way that had nothing to do with dinner. He lowered his gaze then started a conversation—not with me, of course, but with my boobs.

"What's the matter? You're not hungry tonight, sweet thing?"

"I was just listening to you. It sounds like you're *very* good at your business." I struggled to keep the sarcasm from my voice.

"Yes," he said with a slick smile, still talking to my chest, "I'm good at all sorts of things. I could show you exactly how good if you'd like to get out of here and go back to my room at the inn. I'm heading out tomorrow, and it would be a shame if I didn't get to explore all your…assets before I go." His tongue darted out to wet his lips as his gaze raked over me again.

Was he talking to my left boob or my right? I wasn't sure. Or did he want to spend equal time with both of them? The idea of a romp in bed with him had gone from sounding like the perfect romance to a perfect nightmare. I was all for a good time, but not when I had somehow become a headless stick there for his pleasure…and eating carrots. I owned a bakery. Did I look like the kind of girl who restricted myself to carrots? Or was he the kind of man who always ordered for his partner to ensure she kept a *shapely* figure? I would have to ask my breasts because, apparently, they were in charge.

"I think that sounds like… You know what, I'll be back in a minute," I said. "I need to step to the ladies' room."

"Oh. Yeah. Uh, sure," he said, looking annoyed by the delay, but his attention immediately wandered as our waitress, Jessica, passed by. His eyes locked on her green skirt and swaying hips. He didn't even try to hide the way he was undressing her with his eyes. Still staring at Jessica, he had the nerve to add, "We're splitting the check, right? That's what you said, isn't it?"

That was not, in fact, what I had said. For some reason, I had been suffering under the delusion that he might be a gentleman and pay for dinner. Apparently, my breasts were in charge of half of it.

"What do you think, Lefty?" I asked, looking down at my chest. "You got this one covered?"

Grakkar, his eyes still on Jessica's ass, didn't even hear.

Chuckling to myself, I said sweetly, "I'll be right back."

Grabbing my bag and sweater, I approached the back of the restaurant. When I reached the restrooms, I veered right. Slipping behind the servers, I made my way into the kitchen, where I was met with questioning stares. Fortunately, Violet was working. When she saw me, she gave me an empathetic smile.

"Vi, I am so sorry to crash your kitchen," I said.

"No explanation needed," Violet said. "I already saw him, and I definitely heard him. Scoot before he realizes," she said, gesturing to the door.

"Thank you so much," I said, giving her a grateful smile. "Come see me tomorrow. I owe you a scone and a pot of tea! On the house!"

"I'll take you up on that offer!"

I was almost out the door but paused when I passed a tray of the bloomberry tarts.

I turned back to Violet, but she was already laughing. "Take one. You've earned it."

Giving her a grin, I snatched one of the tarts and then fluttered out of the kitchen and onto the cobblestone streets of Moonshine Hollow.

Relieved to be back outside, I took a deep breath and started on my way home.

Enchanted lanterns floated overhead, their fragile colored paper casting rainbow hues on the evening crowds. Moonflowers bloomed in every window box, their iridescent petals unfurling in the darkness and releasing their sweet, dreamy fragrance. It was a beautiful summer night with a full moon and fireflies dancing through the air, their lights mingling with the sparkles of fairy dust that drifted down from the wings of the tiny passing fairies that tended the night-blooming flowers.

Summer had come to Moonshine Hollow once more, and the whole world seemed buzzing with cricket song. A couple walked hand in hand down the street in front of me, passing beneath an arch of moonblush roses that glowed with a soft pink light as they passed by. The evening was warm and sultry, perfect for spending the night with someone you love. Unfortunately for me, Grakkar was *not* someone for me. I hoped that ditching him in the middle of the restaurant would signal that clearly enough.

With a sigh, I fluttered my pale blue wings and drifted back home, munching on the bloomberry tart as I went. At the very least, the tart had been as good as I dreamed. Far better than the date.

I kept an apartment on the floor above my bakery where I lived with the *real* man of my life. Being a pixie afforded certain benefits. I could fly, of course, which meant I didn't need to climb a flight of stairs to get to my second-floor flat. Fluttering upward, I made my way to my slightly cracked window. Pushing it open, I slipped inside.

I was met at once with a questioning meow.

"I know, I know," I said with a defeated sigh. "I'm home early. You don't have to rub it in, Merry."

I snapped my fingers, causing blue sparks to shoot around the room, lighting the candles in my living room. Merry was curled up in his favorite spot at the end of my chaise lounge. Kicking off my heels and dropping my bag and sweater into a chair, I scooped up my caticorn and settled onto the chaise.

"Merry, you may be the only man I will ever truly love. Doesn't that make you happy?"

The cat purred, rubbing his head against me for pats but being careful that he didn't poke me with his little golden horn. He paused, giving himself a little shake before he sneezed. His golden horn glowed brightly for a moment, the effect blinding. When it dissipated, I discovered I was covered in a cloud of multicolored sparkles.

"What the—Merry, are you all right?"

Merry merely blinked, then shook his head, getting out the last of the unexpected sneeze. His golden horn glowed softly as it did when he performed magic. Merry's enchantments mostly consisted of zapping mice or growing iridescent golden wings when he had the zoomies. Sneezing glitter was a new one.

I studied the cat for any signs that he wasn't feeling well—no runny nose, crusty eyes, and he didn't seem overly warm. "Must be the heat of summer," I said, then settled back, absently brushing the glitter away. Merry curled up on my lap as I lay back in the chaise and looked out at the moon.

"Where is my great love story? I want bards to sing about the epic love of Rosalyn Hartwood and her soulmate...the greatest love story of all time. Where is *that* love?" Sighing, I looked down at Merry. "Well, Mer-Mer, it's not happening tonight. Now, where did I leave those triple-chocolate scones?"

CHAPTER 2

BJORN

The blonde-haired beauty on my arm gave me a heated smile, lowering her long lashes and then gazing up at me once more as we twirled around the room. "I am quite adept at all styles of dance, of course. I've trained since I was a young girl. Is there a waltz you prefer?" Ingri asked, beaming a smile that could probably be seen from the southern kingdoms.

"No. I feel equal toward them all," I replied, my true meaning being I disliked them all equally, but I wouldn't be rude enough to say so to the chieftain's daughter. It was not her fault I disliked dancing, loud parties, or rooms packed with people—such as the one I found myself currently trapped in.

The noise in the great hall reverberated off the carved timbers overhead. The king, my father, laughed loudly. His booming laughter filled the entire room and warmed it too, which was no small feat in Frostfjord, where even our summers felt like winter to southern visitors. Pounding his fist on the table, he laughed at a joke one of his men had told him. Beside him, my mother, her long hair pulled into a braid over her shoulder, leaned across the table to speak to Princess Bibka, the frost giantess princess whose family was visiting Frostfjord for trade. My mother's eyes kept darting between me and her target.

I flicked a glance at Princess Bibka. The giantess princess was a beauty with her pale blue skin and long, dark-blue hair, but she looked even more uncomfortable than me. She was, however, precisely the sort of person my mother deemed perfect. Ingri had been my mother's primary target until Bibka arrived.

"So, your wife would have access to all her husband's royal allowance, would she not?" Ingri asked, pulling my attention back with the subtlety of a battering ram. "With that, she could purchase whatever she liked, right? I don't mean to be rude to ask, but my father has always been very sparing with his wealth, and all my dresses are nearly threadbare! Just look," she said, gesturing to her bodice which was decidedly *not* threadbare. She jutted her heaving breasts toward me with such force I nearly had to step back, leaving me wondering how she'd managed to keep them from popping out of the top of her gown. Ingri smiled coyly. "Do you see, Bjorn? I mean, do you *really* see?"

"I..."

She grinned, then exhaled sadly, a practiced pout forming on her lips. "I would want to ensure I looked my best for you at court in Frostfjord. A prince's wife should sparkle as brightly as his treasury, don't you think?"

I smiled politely, but out of the corner of my eye, I saw my mother signaling to the musicians to wrap things up. Thank the Nine Gods.

"I… Yes, I suppose so."

"I knew you would see. I hope you don't find me forward in asking. I'm just a future-minded kind of girl. Are you future-minded, Prince Bjorn?" Ingri asked again, giving me what she clearly thought was a sweet smile and pressing her chest against mine with such determination I feared she might leave an imprint.

Ingri was very beautiful and smelled heavenly, and I was not blind to the allure of her *threadbare* bodice, but in terms of having anything in common, we were somewhere in the negative. Possibly in another realm entirely.

"Well, I…" I began, but blessedly, the reel ended.

I took a step back, giving Ingri a polite bow. "Lady Ingri," I said. "It was a pleasure."

Ingri's brow flexed, a flicker of worry crossing her features as she realized her quarry was about to get away. "Shall we dance the next—"

"Bjorn," my mother's voice called sharply across the hall. "Come."

"If you will excuse me," I told Ingri, bowing to her again, nearly dizzy with relief.

"Of course, Prince Bjorn. Don't stay away for long," she said, blowing me a kiss while her eyes glinted with a coy smile that didn't quite reach their calculating depths.

I turned, catching sight of my family seated at the long

table at the front of the room. My eldest brother, Alvar, was talking with my father and his men, all of them laughing. His wife, Astrid, who regarded my existence with vague notice, was gossiping with her sisters. Beside them, Magnus, my other older brother, was engaged in what looked like a torturous conversation with his new fiancée. It was apparent to everyone but my mother, who had arranged the pairing, that they were a terrible match. Magnus, one of the bravest of our men, looked like he wanted to crawl under the table and hide. I cringed at the sight. My baby brother, Fen, all of fifteen, was too young for my mother's attentions *yet*. He had escaped with a gaggle of other boys his age. They were holed up in one corner of the room comparing their…forearms? What were they doing, exactly? I chuckled lightly, and then my gaze shifted to my younger sister, Asa. When Asa caught my eye, she laughed gleefully at my apparent misery.

I gave her a knowing, *don't laugh, you're next*, look. At eighteen, my sister Asa was Queen Maren's next target once our mother had secured a match for me. Luckily for Asa, I was making things difficult for our mother. Apparently, being uninterested in marriage made you a poor candidate for everyone—except Ingri.

Pulling on a placid smile, I joined my mother.

"Bjorn," my mother said politely. "You will join Princess Bibka for the next dance."

"Of course," I replied, turning to the princess and extending my hand. "Princess."

Princess Bibka gave a grunting assent, took my hand, and joined me on the dance floor.

If anyone thought I was stiff when I danced, they had not seen Princess Bibka. She was…glacial. I smiled. Perhaps I had finally found someone I had something in common with.

"How are you finding Frostfjord, Princess?" I asked.

She paused a long moment, then said, "Hot."

"Yes, I would imagine even Frostfjord is warm for those of you from The Northern Reach."

She didn't reply.

We more veered than twirled around the dance floor. Struggling to find a topic of conversation, I finally said, "I admit I'm not much for dancing or singing. I can warble our royal song, badly, when forced, but I prefer more active hobbies. I spend much time with my father's Master of Horse. I prefer to be outside, tending to our unicorns or on my father's ships. Do you have any hobbies you enjoy?"

She did not respond for so long that I thought she had not heard me. Finally, she said, "No."

"I… What do you enjoy?"

"Sitting."

Struggling for a moment, I finally said, "Yes… I…I also enjoy a good…chair." I flicked my gaze to the princess's family. Alvar had joined them. He was smiling and laughing with Frost Giant King Rarki. They were all cheerful and engaged in animated conversation.

Confused by the stark contrast and worried I had somehow offended the princess, I said, "Princess, I'm sorry, have I done something to—"

"You are the third prince."

"Yes."

"You are too far from the throne. And too short," she told me, then turned and left me on the dance floor.

Clearing my throat and willing my cheeks not to turn red, I mustered up my dignity and rejoined my sister, slipping into the seat beside her.

"What happened? Step on her foot?" Asa asked.

"I'm too far from the throne and too short."

Asa laughed loudly. "So, no rune glow?" she asked, touching my forearm. When Rune elves found their true love matches, the runes deep within us would awaken and glow on our skin.

I huffed a laugh. "Hardly. Maybe I should tell her that Alvar is prone to colds, and Magnus is reckless. By the Nine Gods, if I stay here another minute, I think I'll implode."

"That will be messy. Don't worry, Brother. Mother will find *someone* willing to marry you."

"Ugh," I groaned. "I'm not interested in marrying anyone."

"You sure?" Asa teased, elbowing me in the ribs.

Asa was right. I wasn't being entirely truthful. I wasn't opposed to a partner. I just hadn't found anyone who interested me. Everyone saw me as *Prince* Bjorn. I wanted someone who saw just *me*.

"Okay, well, I am not interested in marrying anyone of Mother's choosing…or sitting in meetings, presiding over festivals, counting coins, or anything else."

"Princess Bibka should be glad you're not the eldest brother. You would make a terrible king. And you'd probably pass a law requiring everyone to keep at least three magical creatures as pets. Where is Smoke, anyway?" she asked, referring to my firewolf.

"Escaped. I told him to save himself while there was still time."

Asa laughed.

I glanced toward my eldest brother, Alvar, who was clapping King Rarki on the back, smiling and laughing. "Alvar will make an excellent king. As for me…" I said, my eyes drifting across the room where I spotted Ingri, who gave me such a sultry look that I felt like I had been physically assaulted. I shuddered. "Be a good sister, and go distract Mother so I can get out of here before she finds someone else for me to marry…or before Ingri pins me in a corner and forces her tongue down my throat while ransacking my pockets."

"And what do I get for my trouble?"

"My goodwill?"

Asa frowned at me.

"How about a packet of peppermint bites from the confectionary in the village," I replied, referring to the confection that could make a person invisible for fifteen minutes, and one of my sister's favorites. "Asa, please. I just need to get away for a moment."

"All right," she said with a soft smile.

Rising, I bent and kissed my sister on her golden hair. "You're still my *least* favorite sibling."

"Obviously."

I slipped away while Asa went to create what I was sure would be the perfect distraction.

Exiting the hall, I was met with a chorus...

"Greetings, Prince Bjorn."

"Honors to you, Prince."

"My prince."

"My prince."

"My prince."

I felt like I was being chased by a flock of formal seagulls.

I responded politely, then escaped down a side corridor and stepped outside.

A soft breeze hit me, wiping away the heaviness of the hall. I breathed deeply, savoring the tang of sea air from the fjord. The smell of the sea breeze cleared my head. I got the same feeling of freedom whenever I visited the countryside. There was nothing quite like the simple pleasure of tending to unicorn herds in complete silence, just enjoying being in their presence.

I made my way down the stone streets toward the harbor, passing shops whose weather-worn signs swung in the breeze. Where the hall was all pomp and ceremony, here were ordinary people living ordinary lives, their laughter genuine and their bows mercifully brief.

A cluster of children huddled on a shop stoop caught my eye—or rather, the suspiciously smoky bundle in one boy's arms did. I recognized a firewolf pup when I saw one, having raised Smoke from the same adorable menace stage.

Glancing about and seeing no sign of my furry troublemaker, I whistled for him. Surely, he was lurking somewhere about, then I went to join the children.

"What do you have there?" I asked, crouching down.

The children looked up, eyes widening. "Prince Bjorn!" the boy holding the pup exclaimed. "Look what my father brought from Smoke Island. A firewolf just like yours!"

"May I?" I gestured to the pup.

The boy nodded and handed the puppy to me.

I lifted him. He already had that familiar glint of mischief in his eyes. He was a tiny thing, all fluff and ember-tipped ears. "Firewolves make excellent companions," I told the boy. "They're fantastic bed warmers in winter but tend to singe your socks if you sleep late."

The boy's eyes grew even wider. "Really?"

"Oh, yes. And once, when I was younger, Smoke set my formal cape on fire right before a big ceremony. The queen was convinced I'd goaded the wolf into it," I said with a grin, knowing that was *exactly* what I had done.

I scratched the pup under his chin, earning a happy yip and a small puff of smoke.

Firewolves were notorious for their ability to breathe fire, their tails becoming pure flame when they were determined to get into trouble. Generally, their magical fire was not dangerous, but they could turn up the heat when they wished. Their dark fur was alive with glowing embers, like coals in a hearth, perfect for the endless winters of Frostfjord. Less ideal for royal wardrobes.

"Do you have a name for this little troublemaker yet?" I asked.

"Cinder," the boy declared proudly.

"Hello, Cinder." The pup licked my chin. "That is an excellent name." I returned him to the boy, who promptly forgot all about me as he and his friends returned to cooing over the pup.

I smiled at the children and then continued on, stopping at the magical confectionery. The shop was full of whimsy and warmth. Every time I stepped inside, I was instantly warmed by the sweet scents. Somehow, the setting was comforting and familiar in a way I couldn't place.

"Is that you, Prince Bjorn?" Mother Urd called from behind the counter.

The confectioner, an ancient woman whose practiced hands had been wrinkled by time, came out of the kitchen to greet me.

"It is, Mother Urd."

She smiled. "Ah, you escaped the hall. How did you manage it?"

"With Asa's help."

"Which means you are here to keep up your end of a bargain. Peppermint bites, then?"

Chuckling, I nodded.

The woman packaged up Asa's sweets then handed them to me. "And these," she added, including a small pack of troll noses. The troll noses, which were cone-shaped confections with a candied shell and a soft, gummy center flavored with elderberries, were my favorite. "I made them this morning. Still your favorite?"

"They are," I said with a laugh, then reached into my coin purse, but Mother Urd waved me away. "A gift, a gift… Princess Asa has already extorted you. This is my way of restoring balance in the world."

Grinning, I took her hand and placed a kiss thereon. "Thank you, Mother Urd."

"You are always welcome, Little Prince Bjorn," she said, then waved to me as she returned to her kitchen.

Popping a troll nose into my mouth, I exhaled a contented sigh and then made my way to the dock. There, the ships creaked against their moorings in the harbor. Vessels came and went between the islands of our kingdom. While the islands offered plenty of opportunities for trading, what I loved most about our lands were the magical creatures. I seized any excuse to sail away to study them, whether it was the uni-seals of Eld Island or the winged reindeer of Frost Isle.

A familiar warm presence at my side announced Smoke's arrival. I patted his head. "And what mischief have you been up to?"

He shook himself, his black fur momentarily sparking with embers.

Turning, I spotted a lanky Sylvan elf, his clothing drastically ill-suited for Frostfjord's *mild* summer weather. He clutched a scroll in one hand and the bindings on his cloak in the other. He hurried down the boardwalk, his gaze set on the great hall.

"Good sir," I called out, "welcome to Frostfjord. You are a stranger here, I think."

The man laughed through chattering teeth. "That obvious? I rarely venture this far north, even in summer, such as I find it here."

I chuckled, then looked the man over. "You're a messenger?"

"Yes, I've come with a message for King Ramr Runeheart, sent from a village called Moonshine Hollow."

"As luck would have it, I'm Prince Bjorn. I can deliver your message to my father," I said, extending my hand to take the scroll, which he passed to me. "Do you have time to join me for a drink?" I offered, gesturing to the nearby alehouse. "Our spiced mead is excellent for warming you from the inside out, and I'd love to hear about your journey."

"Thank you, but I should go before my ship departs for Greenspire. My sister wishes me home for Midsummer. Many salutations to your father, Prince Bjorn," he said, then hurried toward his ship.

I'd barely unrolled the scroll and started reading when a familiar voice piped up behind me. "What's that?" Asa asked.

Pulling the candy from my pocket, I handed her the peppermint bites. "A message from a southern city asking for help with their unicorns. Some odd ailment has affected their herds," I said as I scanned the author's elegant handwriting. Asa read over my shoulder, standing on her tiptoes to see better.

Apparently, the unicorns of Moonshine Hollow had fallen ill, their magic becoming chaotic in ways that had the elders deeply concerned. They'd consulted their local dryad, who had no luck in determining what was wrong. So, they'd turned to us. Rune elves and unicorns had an ancient history together. The unicorn even graced the royal house of Frostfjord's emblem.

While my family shared a passing interest in the creatures, I was the family unicorn enthusiast. My tutor and my father's Master of Horse, Keldor Runeson, had indulged my passion, teaching me everything there was to know about them.

I looked down at Smoke, my mind already churning.

"I know that look," Asa said. "That's your *I've just found an escape* look."

"Hmm," I mused.

Asa grinned. "Mother sent me to tell you that she knows you are trying to hide and that it is not becoming of a prince. She also always wants you to speak to Ingri's father," she said as she studied my face. "But…but maybe I got sidetracked on the way to find you. I was distracted by a particularly interesting…door knob." Asa smirked and then handed me the peppermint bites. "You're going to need these more than me, I think."

"I just need enough time to pack and leave a note explaining that I've gone to Moonshine Hollow on a very princely quest. When they find out I'm gone, maybe you could argue that your *least* favorite brother needs time away to consider the future. Oh, and suggest that maybe they should absolutely *not* send someone after me."

"I might be persuaded…for a price."

"A price? You won't help just because you love me?"

Asa grinned mischievously at me.

"All right. Name it."

"A caticorn."

"A…what?"

"In the Summerlands, they have these adorable little caticorns. They're nothing like our forest cats, who I'm pretty sure are tiny trolls in disguise. The promise of a cute, fluffy caticorn might help me cope with my least favorite brother's absence *and* convince me to convince our mother that you should be left alone. You know I can be very persuasive."

"Blackmail," I said with a grin. "But I'll see to it." I gave my sister a soft smile. "I feel like I'm drowning, Asa. Ingri… I can't imagine a more unhappy life. When she looks at me, all she sees are gold coins. I need to get away where I'm not recognized and just *be* for a little while."

"How are you going to pull this off? Everyone's going to be all 'Prince Bjorn this' and 'my prince' that."

I looked down at the letter. "Not if I'm Bjorn *Runeson*, Master of Horse. I'll book passage south on a visiting ship where I'll go unrecognized. I'll tell the elders of Moonshine Hollow that I was sent by the king."

Asa gave me a soft smile and then hugged me tight. "Be careful," she whispered in my ear.

"And you," I replied, squeezing her. "Don't let Mother set her eye on you while I'm gone."

"I certainly will not." Asa kissed me on the cheek, then slipped from my grasp.

"Still my least favorite," she called, waving to me as she hurried off.

"Still *my* least favorite!" I turned to Smoke. "Well, you menace, are you ready for an adventure?"

Smoke tipped his head to the side, eyeing me curiously, then wagged his tail.

The Summerlands waited, and for the first time in a long while, I felt excited. Let the adventure begin.

CHAPTER 3

ROSALYN

The aroma of orange and thyme lingered in the air as the Crowd Pleaser scones in my oven browned to golden perfection. I inhaled deeply, relishing the sweet smell. I loved baking. Coming up with new magical recipes to nourish my customers and bring peace, comfort, and a little whimsy to *their* lives, filled *my* life with unending bliss. And I didn't mind tasting my creations either. To say I loved sweets was an understatement. Why bother eating if sugar wasn't involved? I was not a plate of carrots kind of girl, no matter what Grakkar thought.

I lifted the order Primrose left for me, checking it again. The Elders of Moonshine Hollow would be meeting today to plan the Midsummer celebration and address any other issues concerning our fair city. Primrose, half-elf caterer extraordinaire, had enlisted me to cater their breakfast.

Crowd Pleaser scones, which always put people in a good mood, were sure to help.

Through my shop window, I saw Primrose entering Winifred's flower store next door. I wished her luck. Winifred would corner her, regaling her with all the town gossip. Hopefully, we'd still make the meeting on time. My nosy but lovable neighbor never missed anything, including somehow already knowing about my spectacularly awful date last night. My blue wings fluttered in annoyance at the memory.

It was half an hour before opening time. Zarina, my apprentice and a promising young kitchen witch, would be here to cover me soon. Once the final batch of scones was ready, I'd have everything prepared for the elders' meeting. I gazed lovingly around The Sconery and Teashop. It had taken time to come together, but now it was the perfect cozy spot. Small round tables topped with vintage tablecloths and old teapots filled with flowers graced the room. Antique teacups hung from the walls, and weathered teapots lined shelves that sparkled with just a hint of pixie dust. My window displayed all my fresh baked goods of the day. From cookies to golden bread loaves to my signature scones, the place exuded what I hoped felt like comfort and love to all my patrons.

This morning, I'd been busy. I'd already brewed several blends of magically refreshing iced tea, mixed teas and herbs for enchanted and comforting hot teas, and baked a dozen varieties of scones—all lovingly made with spells for good vibes of one sort or another. The good thing about being a pixie was that we needed little sleep. We ran differently, which left us with boundless energy. Being a baker was the perfect job for someone like me.

Merry tiptoed along the counter, heading to his warm spot in a basket close to the oven. "And where have you been, you little troublemaker?" I asked. The caticorn ignored me and continued on his way. The magical chime dinged, and I went to the oven, opening the door to reveal the delicious orange-and-thyme scones. I pulled them from the oven and set them on the counter to cool.

As I turned to package up a batch of bloomberry scones, Merry suddenly stopped mid-step. He had a strange look on his face. Was he going to be sick?

"Merry?" I asked. His small horn suddenly glimmered with a blinding light, and he sneezed. A cloud of glittery air enveloped us both. To my confusion and surprise, my orange scones floated off the tray. They glimmered brightly for a moment, lifting just a few inches off the pan, and then, with a popping sound, they dropped back down.

Merry, clearly taken by surprise, arched his back and leaped sideways, looking at me as if this was somehow my fault.

"Merry…"

He arched his back higher and lifted his body up on the tips of his toe beans, his eyes going wide.

"Oh, no, Merry. Please don't."

It was too late.

Merry hopped sideways down the counter and met my gaze.

I knew then I was in for trouble.

He meowed loudly, his glimmering golden wings appearing.

Zoomies.

The shop's bell tinkled as Primrose entered with baskets of shimmering Whisperbloom sunflowers. Winifred followed close behind, carrying a small bouquet of Moonlight Daisies, flowers known for their ability to lift spirits with their soft, pearly glow.

"Rosalyn!" Winifred called cheerfully, her petite gnomish frame peeking around the arrangement. "I thought you could use a little pick-me-up after that date disaster. I have Moonlight Daisies for you. Oh, the nerve of that orc, ruining everyone's dinner. The Kettlestops said everyone is talking about it. Honestly, some people have no sense of proper—"

"Winifred, Primrose, look out!"

Merry made his move.

The caticorn jumped off the counter and began launching himself from table to table, kicking over vases and making chairs teeter. With his little iridescent wings, which only appeared when he had zoomies, he flew around the room at lightning speed. He catapulted off the side of the wall, narrowly missing Primrose and Winifred.

Winifred shrieked, then stepped back.

Careening sideways, Merry caused a broom stand to start to tumble.

I snapped my fingers, sending blue magic to right the stand and the chairs before they hit the floor.

"Merry!" I called, trying to calm him. With all his claws extended, Merry slid across the floor, nearly crashing into

Primrose before catching his footing. Galloping in place for a moment before he finally got traction, he shot toward the storage room. A moment later, I heard the telltale sounds of chaos. I winced with every bang and crash but groaned aloud when I heard a splatter.

"Oh, burnt ends!" I cursed, certain the fresh batch of strawberry marmalade I'd set to cool had just died a terrible death.

"What is going on?" Primrose asked with a laugh, her freckled nose wrinkling as she glanced at the suspiciously sparkly cloud that still lingered. Her curly brown hair seemed to capture some of the glitter, making her look even more magical than usual.

"Merry's magic is acting up. That's the second time he's sneezed and…glitter everywhere. But something else strange happened. I think, maybe, for just a moment—" I began, glancing back at my scones. Had they floated? Was that real? "Whatever it is, he got the zoomies. Sorry about the timing."

"Oh, never mind the caticorn. Caticorns are for sad and lonely girls anyway," Winifred said dismissively as she waved away a lingering cloud of glitter and pulled up a stool at the counter, setting the flowers thereon.

Primrose and I gave one another a knowing look. Winifred didn't have a mean bone in her body, but sometimes her comments cut a little too close.

"What you girls need to focus on is finding a good partner. You are such sweet, charming girls. I can't understand why you aren't married. Now, let me think. I know," she said, snapping her fingers. For a brief moment, an ethereal cloud of pink petals appeared, accompanied by the strong scent of roses. "Primrose, what about that young wizard who opened a shop in the crystal district? He's a handsome one."

Primrose sighed as she settled onto one of the stools. "I had three dates with him last spring. I think... He's too introverted for me," she said, shifting uncomfortably.

"Nonsense."

"He winced when I laughed and got so startled he couldn't stop conjuring frogs. He declined to go out with me again."

"Bah," Winifred said with annoyance. "That boy is too nervous. Good with crystals, bad with people. Rosalyn, have you ever talked to that handsome vampire who runs the midnight market every Hallowmoon? He's something of a beast. That's your type."

I chuckled. "He's handsome, I'll give you that, but I'm a vegetarian, and he's allergic to garlic. It would never work."

Winifred sighed dramatically and began listing more potential suitors—most of whom Primrose or I had already dated or were so unsuitable we couldn't help but laugh. With a defeated sigh, Winifred slipped off her stool. "Mark my words, I'll find better options and have you both married by Yule. Now, have a good breakfast with the elders, dears. Oh, root rot! A town full of beautiful girls and not one suitable bachelor!" she grumbled as she headed away, the door chiming in her wake.

After Winifred left, I handed Primrose a violet-and-white-chocolate croissant—her favorite—and lifted one of my orange-and-thyme scones. "A toast to the sad and lonely caticorn-loving girls?"

Primrose laughed. "Cheers to that! May they long have caticorn hair on their sweaters."

We tapped our confections together, then chewed, savoring the treat and sharing a moment of quiet misery. The daisies on the counter seemed to glow a little brighter, as if encouraging us.

"You know what, Prim?" I said, my blue wings fluttering thoughtfully. "I think we work too much."

"I agree entirely," my friend replied, brushing crumbs from her dress. "I was awake all night going over my calendar and making a schedule for the next, I don't know, six months? Too long, that's for sure."

"We need some sort of adventure," I said. "Something to shake things up. More than just a visit to the Moonlight Springs Spa."

"Agreed," Primrose said, nodding firmly.

"We need to start thinking outside the box," I said, pouring her a cup of tea. "And we need to make the time."

"Sure," Primrose replied with a wry grin. "Right after Midsummer. After that, I'll definitely find a way to make time."

"Same. Right after Midsummer. I'll start thinking about it, too."

"But then we'll have to prepare for the harvest season, Autumn Festival, and Hallowmoon," Primrose reminded me.

"Okay, so we'll do it after that. But then there's Yule.

It's my busiest time of year. So, it'll have to wait until after that."

Primrose's grin widened. "And then we get to Lovers' Day, which kicks off wedding season, which lasts all through spring."

"Okay, after that," I agreed, my wings fluttering as I giggled.

"So, Summer?" Primrose clarified, raising an eyebrow. "Next Summer? As in the current season?"

At that, I laughed hard, then reached under the counter and pulled out a flagon, pouring just a little rosehip cordial into our cups.

"To when we're not too busy to find true love," Primrose toasted, tapping her teacup against mine.

"Cheers to that."

We drank, sighed in unison, and then laughed. As I gazed around my cozy shop and at my equally overworked friend, I realized something. Maybe I'd never find true love, but at least I had good—even if *also* overworked—friends with which to share the journey.

CHAPTER 4

BJORN

The fortnight's journey south transformed the world around me. The dark, churning waters of Frostfjord gave way to the shimmering blue of the southern seas. At Port Silverleaf, Smoke and I boarded a riverboat bound for Moonshine Hollow.

The riverboat carried an array of passengers I'd rarely seen in Frostfjord's isolated realm: a gnomish family chattering excitedly about their relatives, a Sylvan couple with well-worn traveling packs on an adventure, and an orc merchant carefully selecting his seat to balance the small craft. Even the half-elves, halflings, and dwarves aboard spoke of a world far more diverse than the one I'd known. I reveled in the moment.

No one knew me.

I was just another passenger.

I chose a spot at the bow and watched the captain cast an enchantment. With a muttered spell, he summoned a wind that filled the indigo-blue sail, emblazoned with the city's emblem, a wide tree with a full moon on its back. As we glided upriver, a picturesque scene of green with dots of vibrant color unfolded. Whimsy willows with their iridescent leaves dipped their long branches into the water like ladies' fingers trailing on the waves. Tall cattails waved in sheltered covers. Ornery horned goat frogs sat on a log, their beards drifting in the water, watching us suspiciously as we passed.

I closed my eyes, relishing the warmth on my skin.

"What, ho! Cupid swans! Everyone down," the skipper called. His warning had us ducking our heads as we passed a pair of Cupid swans drifting near the bank, their pink feathers luminous in the morning light. At home, Mother would have thrown herself between me and any passing commoner to prevent an enchanted romance. Cupid swans were notorious for zinging love spells at random passersby, causing the victim to fall in love with the next person they saw. Here, I had no queenly mother to protect me. I was just another passenger avoiding the matchmakers' mischief, free to laugh with my fellow travelers at our shared predicament.

Sailing on, we passed white harts grazing in sunlit meadows, their gold-and-silver antlers glinting in the bright sunlight. Spark lilies floating on green lily pads shot tiny fireworks into the air as we passed. And once, I swore I caught a glimpse of a selkie's curious face before she slipped beneath the water's surface.

Soon, farms and homesteads came into view. I spotted a man wearing a tall, pointed gray cap riding in a cart with a halfling. Others walked with baskets in hand as though returning from the village. Before long, the town itself came into sight.

Even from the river, I could tell Moonshine Hollow was a place of charm and wonder. The town sprawled along the riverbank, its cobblestone streets winding past rows of crooked cottages and charming shopfronts. Bridges crossed the river from a dense forest on the other side into the bustling town. Banners depicting the city's emblem hung on lampposts, snapping in the gentle breeze. The buildings were a mix of stucco, stone, and richly engraved wood, with roofs sloping at whimsical angles, many adorned with patches of moss or ivy. Window boxes overflowed with blooms in every imaginable shade, their sweet scent carried on the warm air.

Even from the river, I could see the uppermost limbs of the ancient oak tree at the center of town, its silver-tipped leaves shimmering softly in the sunlight. Along the river was a bustling produce market, with vendors selling fresh fruits, vegetables, flowers, and magical trinkets. A gnome playing the xylophone and a satyr with a guitar entertained passersby as townsfolk chatted, exchanged goods, and waved at passing neighbors. The sound of a distant blacksmith's hammer rang faintly through the air, blending seamlessly with the gentle hum of life around me.

As the riverboat docked, the skipper barked orders and ropes thudded as they hit the wooden pier. The moment I stepped off the gangplank, my senses were overwhelmed in the best way. The aroma of freshly baked bread mingled with the tang of river water and the earthy smell of the fruit market. A soft breeze carried the sound of laughter and the murmur of casual conversation.

A dwarf balancing two wooden crates of vegetables bumped against me as he passed. "Sorry, mate," he said briskly, barely glancing up before moving on.

I couldn't help but smile. No bowing, no murmurs of "my prince," no deferential stares. Here, I was just another traveler, blending into the hum of daily life. The anonymity settled over me like a comforting blanket, and I felt like I could breathe for the first time in years.

The dockmaster waited, checking each of us in with a scroll in one hand and an enchanted feather quill in the other. When he reached me, his eyes traveled upward, noting my tall stature.

"Rune elf?" he asked. "Ah, you must be here about Elder Thornberry's unicorns."

"I am, sir. I'm Bjorn...Bjorn Runeson," I said, taking on the surname of my father's Master of Horse. I swallowed hard, as if keeping down the lie.

"Very good, very good," the man said, gesturing for the quill to make a note.

"I would be much obliged if you could direct me to the elder's house," I added.

The dockmaster waved to a gnomish child sitting atop a barrel nearby. The boy had been occupied with folding a piece of paper.

"Boy!" he called. "Come here. Take this gentleman to Elder Thornberry."

The child hopped off the barrel, his eyes wide when they met mine. "Whoa, I've never met a Rune elf before."

I smiled and ruffled his hair. "I've come from Frostfjord, home of King Ramr Runeheart."

The boy smiled widely and then looked at Smoke. "Sir, your wolf is on fire!"

I chuckled. "He's a firewolf. The flames are merely an enchantment. It's magical fire, not dangerous unless he means it to be. He merely…sparks."

The boy grinned widely, staring at Smoke. "Wow. Okay, come with me."

I handed a coin to the dockmaster and followed the excited child. The boy had folded the paper into the shape of a bird. With a flick of his wrist and a whispered incantation, causing a purple spark, the paper bird floated into the air, its paper wings flapping as if it were alive. It flew ahead of us, turning its tiny head back to check that we followed.

"It's a compass bird," the boy explained proudly. "It'll lead you anywhere you want to go. Do you like it?"

"That is very handy magic," I replied.

"We gnomes always make useful magic," the boy said with a grin.

The compass bird led us to Elder Thornberry's house—or rather, estate. *House* was hardly the correct term for the grand structure. The home was a massive wooden construction with ornate beams, stucco siding, and many balconies adorned with flower boxes overflowing with blooms. It sat at the edge of town, overlooking rolling fields and vineyards. A flower-dotted pond sat before it.

Waterfowl with sapphire-colored feathers, their heads crested with plumes of silver, called to one another as they swam in the tranquil water. Behind the house, I spotted a stable. Fields of bloomberry vines, the bright pink berries glinting in the light, rolled on the slopes beyond the stately home.

"The elder lives here. You should have the compass bird," the boy said, handing me the paper bird. "It will help you find your way around Moonshine Hollow. All you have to do is tell the bird where you want to go, and it will lead you on your way. Except in the rain. Don't use it while it's raining."

"Thank you very much," I said, taking the paper bird from him. "What is your name?"

"Fisk," the child replied with a grin. He was missing his two front teeth.

"A pleasure to meet you, Fisk," I said, bending to shake his small hand. "And thank you for the warm welcome to Moonshine Hollow."

"You're very welcome!" Fisk quipped before dashing off.

Smoke barked once in his wake, causing the child to look back and wave before heading off again.

I folded the bird carefully and tucked it into my pocket.

"You ready to meet the elder?" I asked Smoke, who wagged his tail.

Taking a deep breath, I approached the front door of the house and knocked.

The door opened, and a woman in a bright pink dress appeared. "May I help you?"

"I am Bjorn Runeson. I've come to see Elder Thornberry about the unicorns."

She eyed me over, then smiled. "Oh, of course, of course, from the Frozen Isles! Come in," she said, glancing nervously at Smoke.

"He's housebroken…and fireproof, I assure you."

"Oh, how very enchanting," she said, then gestured for me to follow her inside. "Elder Thornberry is meeting with the other elders. Let me go and tell him you're here. I know they'll all be excited to meet you. Everyone's been so worried about the unicorns."

She led me down the narrow halls decorated with beautiful paintings, the images thereon moving: the clouds rolled across the sky, the trees shook, and the flowers bent in the breeze. The wooden trim within the house was elaborately carved with intricate leaves, flowers, and swirling designs. We finally went to a waiting room with a wide fireplace, cozy-looking chairs, and a large window.

"I'll let them know you're here. Have a seat," she said then opened a door, slipping into an adjoining room. Within, I saw several people seated at a round table.

As I waited for the elder, I went to the window overlooking the vista behind the magnificent house. The hills behind the manor rolled with bloomberry vines. As well, there were vast stretches of green hills dotted with wildflowers where horses grazed. I smiled at the sight, vastly different from the frozen waters and icy tundra of the mountains around Frostfjord. I exhaled deeply, feeling something unknot inside me, releasing a tension I felt like I'd been holding my entire life.

Beside me, Smoke whined happily and then pawed my hand. "You feel it too?"

The door opened behind me, and a man appeared. A halfling man crossed the room, his hand extended. He was finely dressed, wearing a handsome brocade robe and a small, pointed cap with a tassel hanging from its end.

"Bjorn Runeson, is it?" he said, smiling broadly as he shook my hand vigorously. "Well met. Well met. I am Elder Thornberry. It's a great pleasure to meet you here, far from the frozen north. It has been quite a journey for you, hasn't it?"

I took his hand in a firm shake and gave a slight bow. "Sir. Indeed, but I was delighted to leave the cool winds behind and be greeted by your warm summer breezes."

Elder Thornberry laughed heartily. "We're grateful to King Ramr for sending you," he said then looked at Smoke. "And you are?"

"This is Smoke, my firewolf."

"Handsome boy," he said with a smile. "We are so glad to have you here. As I mentioned in my letter, we are dealing with a mysterious illness that has afflicted our unicorns. They graze deep in the valley, out in the hills," he said, gesturing toward the window, "but we've brought in a mare and her foal, who seem particularly affected. They're in the stables. Let's have a look…after breakfast."

"Given the urgency of the situation, perhaps I should—"

"Nonsense, my boy. I can't expect you to work on an empty stomach. And you haven't lived until you've tried the baked goods from The Sconery. Rosalyn—she's the baker—has magic in her hands. Come. It's been a long voyage. Come and eat. And we'd best hurry up. The other elders have already gone in. They may be all prim and proper, but they eat like wolves when the Sconery is involved," he said with a laugh, then turned to Smoke again and added, "No offense to your good boy here, of course."

I had to admit, I was feeling very hungry. I had not eaten since the ship from Frostfjord, and the food had been meager fare even then. "Very well. Lead the way, sir."

"Good. Good. Come," the elder told me, taking my hand. "Onward, my boy, to love at first bite!"

CHAPTER 5
ROSALYN

I stood beside Primrose, my arm linked with hers, as we surveyed our work. The bright Whisperbloom sunflowers Winifred had provided brightened the room and added a calming, peaceful atmosphere that encouraged cooperation. Enchanted peace candles from Lilibet, our local candlemaker, added to the atmosphere of peace. Primrose had stationed an enchanted harp in one corner. It played pleasing, calm songs. At the center table, I had set out the baked goods, all imbued with enchantments for team-building, camaraderie, cooperation, and humor. On a stand in the corner, I'd placed the beverages, blends mixed for concentration and elevated intelligence, alongside my favorite teacups I'd brought just for the occasion.

"Everything looks perfect," I told Primrose.

Primrose, a half-elf with a human father and Sylvan elf mother, had an unusual form of magic. She created comfort. As well, she was able to synthesize others' gifts, melding them together. That ability made her the perfect caterer. Even now, a soft golden glow hung in the air.

"Are you sure?" Primrose asked worriedly, chewing the corner of her lip nervously.

I wrapped my arm around her waist and pulled her close. As her best friend, I knew very well that Primrose always felt uncertain. She felt like everything she did was too much or not quite right.

"It's perfect. Just like every event you manage. My heart feels perfectly at ease," I told her in truth. "I need you to come by and fix my apartment again."

Primrose chuckled, then exhaled heavily, releasing some of her tension.

The doors to the meeting hall opened, and the elders entered, all talking in a loud hubbub.

Primrose gave me a knowing look, then flicked her fingers toward the harp, enhancing its volume just a little so it could be heard over the gabbing crowd.

The semi-heated discussions and disagreements soon faded when the elders started to take in the room, the enchantments working on them. Their bickering was replaced by pleasantries and warm smiles.

"And that's my cue," Primrose said. Patting my shoulder, she left my side and went to greet the elders. "My illustrious elders," she began, welcoming them to the brunch.

Leaving her to it, I went to the tea station once more. I began adjusting the cups and saucers, ensuring I had everything ready.

"You don't see me," a voice said jokingly from beside me as Emmalyn, Elder Thornberry's daughter, appeared. Grinning at me, she filled a traveling canteen with Pink Blossom tea. "I'm risking having to socialize because of the lure of your scones. I just wanted you to know."

I grinned at the pretty blonde, whom I knew to be far more interested in her horses than anything her father might wish her to attend to, as she wrapped one of my scones into a napkin and slipped it into her hip pouch.

"Good to see you too, Emmalyn."

Emmalyn laughed. "Everything smells amazing, Rosalyn. Tell Primrose I said it looks beautiful. I'll see you at book club tomorrow?"

I grinned and nodded. "Did you like *Crown and Crumpets*?" It had been my turn to select the book for our group, and I had gone with my absolute favorite classic.

"Chef's kiss," she told me, gesturing in tandem, then let out an "eek" when, from the other room, I heard the sound of her father's voice.

"Must escape," she said, then snapped her fingers, suddenly turning translucent.

"I can still see you with my pixie vision." Which was true, even if it was a vague shimmering outline.

"Good thing halflings don't have that," she said with a grin. "If my father asks, you never saw me."

And with that Emmalyn disappeared down a side hallway and out of sight.

I chuckled and turned back.

When I did, my breath caught in my chest.

Beside the elder was a hulking man I had never met

before. His rugged dress with an open-necked tunic, kilt, and fur-trimmed leather vest gave him away at once as an outsider, but it was the firewolf at his side that confirmed who he was—Rune elf.

"Friends, friends," Elder Thornberry called, gesturing to everyone. "May I introduce Bjorn Runeson, Master of Horse for King Ramr of Frostfjord. He came from the far frozen reaches to see our unicorns. Let us give him a welcome!"

At that, the elders clapped politely.

Reminding myself to breathe, I also gave a polite clap.

Bjorn, who looked entirely uncomfortable, set his hand on his waist and gave the room a very practiced formal bow. When he rose, his eyes scanned the room, pausing when he saw me. He met my gaze for a moment.

Taken by surprise, my wings fluttered, sending a glimmer of sparkles around me.

I gave the stranger a soft smile and inclined my head to him.

He blinked, rubbed his forearm, then gave me a brief smile before looking away.

My cheeks burning, I turned and began filling the cups on my tray as my mind began spooling out romantic visions of myself and the Rune elf. Taken so off guard by my thoughts, I was surprised to find my hands shaking. I spilled the tea onto the saucers.

Oh, burnt ends! Concentrate, girl.

I cleaned up the mess then sent the serving tray around the room, floating on a cloud of glimmering blue light. I then prepared another tray. When I had it ready, I turned to send it off but pitched to an awkward stop when I found myself face to face with a firewolf. The giant canine wagged his tail, the fiery plume spewing magical embers.

I fluttered my wings quickly working to right myself as the teacups nearly went careening toward the floor.

Then, someone stepped forward, grabbing the other side of the tray to prevent a near disaster. As I leaned, I heard the tell-tale clack of porcelain hitting too hard…a sound that told me I'd definitely chipped or broken something. "Oh no," I muttered.

Righting myself, I looked up to find a hulking figure holding my tray in place.

The Rune elf.

"Oh, thank you! I…" My cheeks burned redder than a Midsummer fire. *Oh my gods, what is wrong with me?* "Thank you. I nearly lost the whole tray," I said with a laugh, setting in on a nearby table.

"My apologies. Smoke has the uncanny ability to detect the person most likely to feed him."

"Well, I'm the baker, so his instincts are perfect," I said then set the tray aside. "I'm Rosalyn, by the way," I said, extending my hand. "You are very welcome in Moonshine Hollow, Mister Runeson."

"Just Bjorn," he replied, smiling softly as he took my hand and placed a genteel kiss thereon.

I'm going to die.

Right here.

In the middle of breakfast.

I am going to literally implode into a cloud of glitter.

I laughed nervously. Desperate to not make a fool out of myself, I turned back to the firewolf.

"Smoke, is it? Well, you must be a very smart boy to know who has cookies for dogs." Sticking my hand into my apron pocket, I produced three small dog cookies. I turned to Bjorn. "Okay, before you judge a lady for carrying dog cookies in her pocket, there is a pega-poodle that lives on the corner before the elder's house. I always bring a cookie or two for him when I come this way. Do you mind?" I asked, meeting the Rune elf's gaze.

His eyes were colored cool gray flecked with shades of blue like a dark sea in a storm.

Bjorn nodded, then rubbed his forearm once more.

Smiling, I turned back to Smoke. "Wily boy," I said, handing the wolf the treats, which he took politely.

I clapped off my hands and turned to Bjorn again. "And what can I get for you? Pink blossom tea? Maybe Midsummer blend? It's my specialty brew," I said, gesturing to the tray. "Midsummer pairs very nicely with my orange-and-thyme scones," I said, then reached for a teacup. Then, I saw my favorite cup, the one with pretty pink butterflies painted on the side. Its handle was broken. "Oh, burnt ends," I whispered, frowning. Sadly, I set it aside and reached for another, topping it off with Midsummer tea, which I handed to Bjorn.

When I gave the cup to the Rune elf, our fingers brushed as the cup passed between us.

When they did so, Bjorn gasped lightly. For the flicker of a second, I saw a sparkle of blue illuminate on his forearm.

Confused, I merely smiled. "Is my pixie magic working on you already?"

Bjorn looked at me, a mix of confusion and horror on his face, then set the cup down and turned and walked away.

Puzzled, my wings fluttered with annoyance.

Smoke whined, pawing gently at me.

"Was it something I said?" I asked.

The firewolf wagged his tail, came in for a head pat, then trotted off behind his master.

Confused, I pushed the odd encounter aside and then made my way around the room, passing out drinks and using my magic to keep the teapots pouring. The elders snacked on my confections, and everyone laughed and joked, warmed by Primrose's magic and the enchantments in my scones. I eyed the Rune elf, who stood politely beside Elder Thornberry. When a small mob of the elders surrounded him, peppering him with questions, I could see the struggle behind his eyes. He wanted to escape. While his physical mannerisms were kept in check—perfect posture, respectful nods, and polite smile—his eyes told a different tale.

I paused a moment to study him. I had taken his abrupt departure as rudeness, but was that really it? Maybe I had just overwhelmed him. Had he gotten overstimulated? This whole scene was a lot, and he was from another culture, another city.

Primrose, who had been busy working the room, finally joined me.

"It's going well, I think," she said.

I nodded. "Yes, the elders seem very happy."

"Yes, they do. Thank goodness," she said, then followed my gaze. "I see you didn't miss that tall mug of ale."

"I never thought it was possible to spontaneously combust in response to someone's sex appeal, but I think I was dangerously close."

Primrose chuckled.

"I've already envisioned him charging in on a white horse to whisk me away to some romantic cabin where all the ravishing will occur."

"Of course."

"Unfortunately, my imaginings must have reached my eyes, and I'm pretty sure I scared him off."

"How so?"

"Well, he kind of…ran away from me," I said, then laughed. "Oh my gods, Primrose, he literally turned around and walked away from me mid-conversation," I said, feeling my stomach drop. "I'm doomed. Cursed. Forsaken by the gods. Maybe my mother's right. Maybe I should return to Spring Haven and settle down with a nice pixie man. First Grakkar, and now this? The first *truly* interesting man to step into Moonshine Hollow and… Maybe I had hearts floating around my head. Do I seem desperate? I feel desperate."

Primrose gave me a sympathetic smile. "I'm sure that wasn't it."

I studied Bjorn once more.

He leaned down and spoke to Elder Thornberry in a low tone.

"Right, right," the elder said. "Friends, I must see Bjorn to the unicorns now."

Bjorn smiled with what looked like relief.

"The rest of you, enjoy the breakfast. Delicious as always, Rosalyn! And very beautiful, Primrose," the elder called, garnering our attention.

I gave the elder a polite smile.

When I looked toward Bjorn, he was already headed out the door. Smoke, however, paused and looked back at me.

I waved to the wolf, who wagged his tail, and then I sighed heavily.

"Well, at least the wolf liked you," Primrose said with a laugh.

I gave her a mock scowl. "Not funny."

Feeling frustrated with myself, I made my way around the room, refilling cups once more. By the time the elders were done and moved back to the meeting room, all the scones had been devoured, the tea finished, and nothing was left but dirty cups and crumbles.

Primrose and I got to work packing up our goods, and the elder's helpers carried our supplies to a wagon waiting out front. I was packing up the last of the teacups when I discovered something off. The teacup with the broken handle sat where I'd left it, but now, the cup was intact. Confused, I lifted it carefully and inspected the cup. There was no sign of a crack. In fact, it looked as if it had never been damaged.

My brow furrowed.

"Ready?" Primrose asked.

"I… Yes. I think so," I said, setting the pink cup into the wicker basket.

Primrose nodded, turned to my trunk, and whispered quietly as she waved her hand over the cups. A warm pink glow enveloped them. "That should keep them comfy for the ride home. After all that excitement, I need a drink. You?"

"I've been dreaming of a lemon smash."

Primrose grinned. "The Surly Dragon it is. Another event complete, a sack of coins in my pocket, and it's sing-along night. Let's go."

As we exited the elder's house, I craned my neck to look toward the stables. No sign of Bjorn.

Primrose chuckled. "Don't worry. If it's true love, you'll see him again. Next time, however, try not to undress him with your eyes."

"But it's just so hard not to, and I have a very good imagination."

Primrose laughed.

And with that, we made our way into town, my heart beating a little harder every time I thought about that Rune elf, my mind playing dangerously with what-ifs. Prim was right. If it was meant to be, I'd bump into him again. And if not, I'd have to toss him on the heap with Grakkar and all my other false hopes.

One day, my Lord Thornwick would arrive.

One day…

CHAPTER 6

BJORN

Elder Thornberry talked nonstop as we strolled from the house to the stables. Rightly proud of his farm, he pointed out all the beautiful sights. I tried to listen, but my mind went again and again to my encounter with the pixie. I had never met a pixie before, and as it turned out, they were as beautiful and charming as their reputation suggested. But when she beamed that warm smile at me, it triggered an immediate and illogical reaction.

She was smiling at *Prince* Bjorn.

She was friendly and playful with *Prince* Bjorn.

She was being kind and a little flirtatious because I was *Prince* Bjorn.

And then…my runes glowed.

What in the Nine Gods was that?

Never, ever had my runes shown any reaction to a woman.

By the time I reminded myself that she had no idea I was *Prince* anything, it was too late. Embarrassed by my rude behavior, all I wanted to do was escape. But before I found my exit, I watched her interact with the others. She was just…nice. She was kind, smiley, and seemingly well-loved by everyone in the room.

And I had acted like a bore.

Hell, even Smoke had been more cordial to her. Leave it to my firewolf. He was never wrong about people.

I only hoped that fixing her teacup would cheer her.

My stomach knotted when I realized I'd been very rude to the most beautiful woman I had ever seen in my entire life: red hair, wide blue eyes, a sweet button nose, and an endlessly kissable mouth. She was—

"Do you like bloomberry wine?" Elder Thornberry asked, interrupting my thoughts.

Perfect.

She is perfect.

"Honestly, sir, I've never tasted it," I admitted. "We favor ale and mead in the north."

"Well, I'll ensure you have a bottle while you're here. My family bottles the finest bloomberry wine in all of the Summerlands," he said proudly.

"I would be honored."

The elder smiled widely.

Was everyone in Moonshine Hollow this welcoming? People were always crowding around me in Frostfjord, but their intentions had not always been so pure. Here, people just seemed interested in meeting me.

Me.

This was the very reason I'd come here.

I needed to get out of my own way.

We arrived at the stables, a large building suitable for housing at least a dozen horses. Inside, I noticed stable hands working diligently and a young woman with flowing blonde hair brushing a horse. She paused when she saw us, craning her neck to see what was going on.

I followed Elder Thornberry to the back. There, a unicorn mare and her foal had been housed. The unicorns we had in the north were vastly different from the creatures before me. In the Frozen Isles, they were shaggy creatures with coats of gray, brown, or black and steel-colored horns. These unicorns were far more dazzling. Their coats were silky white, with manes and tails that shimmered with streaks of rainbow colors, their golden horns glistening in the stable's soft light. They reminded me of the nykur, mythical creatures from our northern legends. Yet, some claimed they still roamed deep in the Frozen Isles. When I was a boy, I thought I'd once spotted one, but the creature vanished when I tried to move in for a better look.

"Elder Thornberry," I said, turning my attention back to him, "tell me more about the affliction facing your unicorns. In your message, you mentioned chaotic magic. Can you explain what you mean?"

Elder Thornberry gestured to the foal. "It comes in fits and starts. You just never know what's going to happen. One moment, everything's fine, and then they stamp their hoof or shake their mane, and that horn lights up. Then…chaos."

"What do you mean?"

As if on cue, the foal started prancing about his stall. He whinnied and kicked, and then there was a sudden blast of light from his horn. I winced at the bright light. The whole barn glowed. Afterward, a loud protest erupted, accompanied by the frantic clucking of chickens. I turned to see the chickens that had been pecking through the straw now suspended four feet off the ground, encased in shimmering golden halos. They flapped and shook, trying desperately to free themselves from whatever magic had gripped them, but to no avail.

Then, as abruptly as it began, the spell dissipated with a peculiar zapping sound. The golden orbs holding the chickens vanished, and they dropped to the floor in a flurry of feathers, squawking indignantly.

"Chaos," Elder Thornberry said, gesturing.

"I see," I said as I watched the chickens hurry from the stables, clucking loudly in indignation.

"The effects are less pronounced in the mare, though she managed to turn an entire trough of water into ice and summon a tiny snow flurry," Elder Thornberry explained.

"And the same thing is happening with the other unicorns? The herd in the fields?" I asked.

Elder Thornberry nodded gravely. "Yes, all manner of chaos is unfolding out in the fields. My Master of Grove is concerned about the bloomberries. We don't want something to happen that disrupts the wine harvest this fall. But, as much as I worry about the wine, I'm far more troubled for the poor unicorns and what this may mean."

"Understandable," I said, glancing at the mare and foal. "I will observe this pair but should also visit the herd."

Elder Thornberry nodded. "I'll make arrangements for someone to take you out tomorrow. There is a small cabin out in the fields where you can stay, but for now, I have a room for you here in the house. It's quiet and private, with plenty of space for a northerner to stretch out."

"That's very generous, sir," I replied, "but you don't have to. I can easily stay in a lodging in town."

"I'll hear no debate. You've come a long way to help us, and you'll need a good place to rest. Now, I'm off to rejoin the elders. My daughter, Emmalyn, who's been listening to this entire conversation, will be sure you find your way. Right, Emmalyn?"

"Of course, Father," came a cheerful reply from nearby. The blonde-haired girl I'd noticed earlier appeared, smiling warmly.

"Let her know if you need anything," Elder Thornberry added with a grin. "And good luck to you."

With that, the elder left, leaving me alone with the unicorns and Emmalyn's curious gaze. I stepped into the stall, moving slowly and deliberately. The mare watched me cautiously, her ears swiveling in my direction. The foal, however, was more curious about Smoke. He poked his head over the stall gate and his nostrils flared as he tried to determine what, exactly, Smoke was.

I whispered softly as I moved close to the mare, keeping my voice calm and steady. Rather than rushing to touch them, I let them sniff my hands and observe me from a safe distance. I knew trust was built slowly and caution was paramount with their magic acting unpredictably.

"Any signs of injury?" Emmalyn asked, leaning against a beam as she watched.

"None that I can see," I replied, glancing over the foal's coat. "No swelling, no strange markings, no obvious sources of pain. Whatever's affecting them seems...deeper. I'll need time to understand it."

Her expression turned serious. "The dryad who came to examine them thought the same. He tried giving them a draught of moonshine to stabilize their magic, but it didn't help. Poor creatures. They look so unsettled. It's heartbreaking to see them like this."

I nodded, taking note of the foal's restless movements.

Emmalyn reached into her pocket and pulled out a small cloth sack. The unicorns' ears perked up instantly. "This will help make friends," she told me. "Sugar blossom cubes never fail." She handed the bag to me.

Within, I found cubes glowing faintly with a soft pink shimmer and giving off a faintly floral scent. The mare and foal eyed the sack eagerly, their noses twitching. I chuckled then offered one cube to the foal and another to the mare. They accepted eagerly, chewing contentedly before nudging me for more.

"See? Works every time," Emmalyn said with a knowing smile.

I smiled, gave each unicorn another cube, and gently stroked their necks. Their tension seemed to ease, if only slightly. "Thank you," I said, turning back to her. "These are remarkably effective."

"I imbue them with calming herbs. Keep them," she said lightly.

"Thank you."

"I'm four stalls down if you need anything. Try not to get impaled. It would look badly on my family if we killed a visiting representative from King Ramr's court."

I chuckled. "I'll try my best. I'm Bjorn, by the way."

"Emmalyn," she replied. "Yell if you need me."

I returned my focus to the unicorns. The mare and foal were watching me, their eyes flicking toward the bag in my hand. Smiling, I offered them another cube each, then gently stroked their silky necks.

"You see, my friends," I murmured, "I'm here to help you. And, in your own way, you're helping me too. You just don't know it."

The mare nickered softly. As the sunlight streamed into the stall, warming the space with golden light, I felt a quiet sense of purpose settle over me. Whatever was happening here, I would do everything in my power to set it right. No one needed to call me *Prince* Bjorn, dress me in an uncomfortable doublet, force me to sing royal songs, or make me dance with women I was not interested in to make that happen. Here, I was *just* Bjorn. And *just* Bjorn would solve the riddle of the ailing unicorns.

I SPENT THE REST OF THE MORNING AND INTO THE LATE afternoon tending to and observing the unicorns. On two occasions, the mare evoked cold weather. Once, a flurry swept through the barn, covering everything in snow. On the second occasion, she sneezed, filling her stall with a foot of powdery white snow. On both occasions, her horn had lit up before the blustery weather. The same was true for the foal. But his magic was far more random. It went from making rose vines appear and disappear to a sneeze that refilled everyone's buckets with oats. There was no rhyme or reason for his affliction, and from what I could see, there was no stimulus for it either. Nothing had changed. Nothing had excited them. In fact, the foal had been dozing when the oats incident happened. I talked with the grooms, inspected the unicorns' feed, and looked for possible allergens but found nothing. I felt that the answer I was looking for would be found in the fields beyond where the rest of the herd roamed.

Smoke was the first to alert me to how much time had passed with his usual hungry dances.

"Hungry, eh?" I asked the wolf. "Shall we see what Moonshine Hollow has to offer?"

The wolf, sensing a meal was coming, wagged his tail and jumped excitedly.

Chuckling, I pulled out the compass bird the gnome child had given me.

"My wolf companion and I need some dinner. Will you kindly lead the way?"

The paper bird shook itself like a real bird and then set off, leading us off Elder Thornberry's property and back toward Moonshine Hollow. We wove down the winding streets, passing many quaint shops where people paused to chat with one another. The bird led me on meandering loops, down alleys and streets with crooked little two-story houses, gardens, and magical window displays. Enchantments had been set on many of the goods for sale, including a loom weaving a design on its own accord and a paintbrush painting, and then magically erasing, images as people passed. When I paused to watch, the brush considered me and then quickly painted a picture of a gray, tossing sea filled with icebergs.

"Very well done," I told the paintbrush, giving it a smile and nod.

Happy sparks effervesced around it before it erased my image and moved on to the next design.

The little paper bird led me down one lane and then another. Soon, the scent of freshly baked bread filled the air.

My stomach growled hungrily.

The bird fluttered to a stop and alighted on my shoulder.

I turned to discover I was standing before The Sconery and Teashop. A wooden sign on which the shop name was depicted, decorated with hand-painted flowers, swayed in the breeze. On the sidewalk outside the café, people sat at small tables enjoying drinks and food. A glimmering chalkboard sign outside displayed the *Evening Specials*, which included varieties of hearty soups, baked savory pies, and breads. Inside, I saw Rosalyn fluttering about her shop. She was refilling glasses with a sparkling drink with lemon slices and lavender sprigs. The soft glow of the dying sunlight painted shades of pink and gold on the flowers outside her windows. They shimmered with golden light, perfectly framing the luminescent beauty of the woman within.

Here?

The bird led me here?

Once more, I felt a warm tingle on my skin. I looked down to see the blue runes on my forearm sparking to life.

I watched as the pixie stopped and chatted with her customers, all smiles and pleasantries. She was a pure beauty and kind of heart. I'd never met anyone like her before.

"Well, are you going in or not?" a small voice asked, pulling my attention away.

I turned, finding a gnomish woman in a massive straw hat, flowers adorning her chapeau, fixing me with a penetrating stare.

"I…"

"I don't know you," the gnomish woman said, her gaze narrowing. "Are you traveling through?"

"Yes, ma'am," I said politely, suddenly feeling unnerved and worried Rosalyn might see me standing in the middle of the street, gawking at her. If that happened, I might just die of embarrassment. I took the paper bird from my shoulder and carefully stuffed it into my pocket. "If you'll excuse me," I said, then looked down at Smoke. "Come on, boy," I said, then hurried down the street, looking over my shoulder once more, watching as the gnome woman fixed me with such a stare that I felt guilty.

When I turned the corner, I laughed.

Never in my life had anyone made me feel like such a scoundrel.

"I expected many things would happen when I wasn't *Prince* Bjorn, but being treated like a common criminal by a lady in a flowered hat was not one of them," I told the wolf with a laugh, and then we headed back into town. At a vendor barbequing meat at a small stand along the river, I purchased Smoke a hefty piece of beef he chewed on while I watched the boats float by. I sat quietly, minding my business and enjoying the warm breezes as the sun set. Finally, when it grew dark again, I took the compass bird from my pocket.

"Okay, for real this time. The wolf is fed. Now, I need something to eat."

Once more, the compass bird took off and flew back down the winding roads of the village. I was grateful to the gnomish boy who had gifted me the enchantment. I had no idea where I was, and the streets of Moonshine Hollow rarely followed any predictable pattern. We climbed up a set of stairs and then turned down a street, the bird fluttering before me as it stopped. Coming from a different direction, I hadn't realized where I was until…

First, I smelled the bread.

And then I saw the sign.

The Sconery and Teashop.

Once again, I was standing outside Rosalyn's café.

Inside, she was tidying up for the night. Three enchanted brooms swept while she fluttered around the space. I looked more closely when I realized she had something fluffy hanging from one arm. She patted the little creature and then set what I realized was a caticorn on the counter. She had a whole conversation with the caticorn and then turned to clean again.

Again, the compass bird alighted on my shoulder.

"Very funny," I told the bird.

A bell over the flower shop door beside Rosalyn's café chimed. Once more, the gnomish woman appeared.

"You again," she said with a scowl.

"I…"

"Do I need to call the constables? What do you want around here? Why are you watching—"

"Bjorn?" Rosalyn called softly.

Please, Lord of Lightning, send a bolt and strike me dead.

Kill me here on this street.

Eviscerate me.

"I…" I began, and then the compass bird lifted off my shoulder and fluttered toward Rosalyn, looking back at me. "A child gifted me with the compass bird. I told it I was hungry and…" I explained awkwardly.

"Rosalyn, do you know this stranger?" the gnomish woman asked, eyeing me suspiciously.

"Yes, I do. He's a friend of Elder Thornberry," Rosalyn answered simply. "Come in, Bjorn. I'm just closing up for the night, but I have lots of soup and fresh bread left."

"I don't mean to impose, I just—"

"Was hungry?" Rosalyn asked with a light laugh and a smile that made something in my stomach unknot. "That's what a café is for, you know. Come."

"Rosalyn, this man has been lingering outside your door," the gnomish woman said, giving me a fierce look.

"It's all right, Winifred. He seems harmless. As for

you," she said, turning to Smoke, "are you a nice boy with kitties?"

"He is," I reassured her.

"Then, come. I have more cookies," she told Smoke, who wagged his tail. "'Night, Winnie," she called to her neighbor, who gave me a suspicious huff.

I looked down at Smoke. "Mind your manners," I said, then grinned at my own feelings, "and I'll mind mine."

Rubbing my forearm, I cleared my throat, pushed back my hair, and headed inside.

Lady of Spring, be with me...and please, do not let me make a fool of myself.

CHAPTER 7
ROSALYN

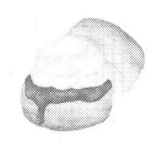

Even though I was smiling, it was very possible the butterflies in my stomach were going to burst out and kill me, causing a grizzly scene that would scar Bjorn for life.

I held the door open for the Rune elf and his firewolf.

Merry immediately paused his grooming and looked at the firewolf with suspicion.

The wolf had a similar reaction, but he was more excited than aggressive. He whined excitedly and wagged his tail quickly, doing a little hop in interest.

Bjorn smiled apologetically. "He's good with cats, I promise. He endlessly follows them around our stables, trying to play with them or groom them and thoroughly annoying them in the process."

"He has good-boy energy," I said with a laugh.

And so do you, Mister Runeson.

I took a pet cookie from a jar on my counter and

tossed it to the wolf. "Please, have a seat," I told Bjorn, gesturing to the last table upon which I hadn't yet stacked the chairs. "You see. It was meant for you," I said, trying not to let Bjorn see the heart shapes in my eyes.

"Thank you. I really don't mean to put you out. The compass bird…" he said, gently lifting the compass bird from his shoulder with care as if it were alive. "It kept bringing me here. Your neighbor must have thought I was stalking you."

"Winifred is suspicious of everyone, but she is also the one person in town who knows all. If there is any mystery to unfold, she will get to the bottom of it," I said with a light laugh.

Bjorn's brow furrowed slightly. "I see."

Interesting. "So, how about a bowl of summer squash soup and a farmer's pie?"

"That sounds amazing. Thank you, Rosalyn."

"My pleasure," I replied, my stomach twisting at the sound of my name spoken in his northern Rune elf accent.

Snapping my fingers, I set a cup, saucer, and a pot of tea coasting on clouds of glimmering blue light across the room to Bjorn. By chance, I had just brewed a pot of Evening Relaxation. The enchantment poured him a cup while I prepared his dinner.

"So, the compass bird kept bringing you here?" I asked.

"Yes," Bjorn replied with a light chuckle.

I set the pie in the oven to warm and ladled out the soup.

"It *kept* bringing you here," I said with a grin. "So, why

didn't you come in the first time?" I asked, arching a playful eyebrow.

"Oh, I…" he said, then rubbed the back of his neck nervously, inadvertently flexing his enormous bicep that strained against the fabric of his shirt. Something low in my belly clutched at the sight, and I had to drown the whirlwind of images that wanted to bubble up in my mind.

"You…?" I asked leadingly.

"Well, I just didn't want you to think I was being…insistent."

Please be insistent. "Never doubt a compass bird. They know exactly where you're supposed to be. Cream or sugar for your tea?"

He shook his head.

"Purist. I see," I said with a laugh. "Now, tell me all about your voyage here. I want to hear everything."

"Truly?" he asked, a genuine note of surprise in his voice.

"Of course. Why wouldn't I?"

His manner relaxing, Bjorn began to tell me all about his adventures, from leaving the Frozen Isles to traveling across the open sea. I worked in the kitchen as he shared the tale. There was excitement in his voice. It was clear that he loved an adventure. I had just taken the farmer's pie from the oven when he mentioned the Cupid swans on Silver River.

"Oh, they are a menace." I laughed. "They nearly caused one of our eldest elder couples to divorce last year!

Luckily, Juniper, she's the herbalist in Moonshine Hollow, was able to make a draft to rescue them from the enchantment. Still, it was all the town could talk about for days. Elder Nona, well into his hundredth year, was voyaging upriver when he got caught in the Cupid swan's spell. He fell in love with a human bard and tambourine player named Prissy Stockings, who was traveling on the same riverboat. The girl was barely twenty years old," I said with a laugh. "Poor thing, she didn't want to embarrass Elder Nona, but he pursued her earnestly," I said, setting Bjorn's food before him. "Elder Nona's wife was furious and threatened to roast the Cupid swans for dinner." Going to the bakery case, I arranged a plate of cookies and petit-fours, then settled in across from Bjorn, pouring myself a cup of tea. "Once the enchantment was undone, Elder Nona spent the next year earning his wife's forgiveness. I'd feel sorry for him, but he kept me and Winifred in business. Weekly orders of rainbow zinnias from Winnie and chocolate drop roses from me—both his wife's favorites. And poor Prissy Stockings never performed in Moonshine Hollow again," I said, then laughed, Bjorn joining me.

Bjorn watched me carefully as I added my rose-enhanced sugar to my cup. I was on the fifth teaspoon when I saw him grin.

"It's a pixie thing," I lied.

"Is it?" he asked with a playful eyebrow raise.

Chuckling, I shook my head. "No. It's a decidedly Rosalyn Hartwood thing. Did you think this plate of desserts was for both of us?" I asked, pulling it toward me, selecting a purple cassis-flavored petit-four, and taking a bite.

Bjorn laughed. Setting down his spoon, he dipped into his hip bag.

"They may be a little squished," he said, "but try them," he said, setting a package of cone-shaped confections before me.

"Thank you," I said, lifting the packet. "What are they?" I asked with a laugh.

"Troll noses," he replied with a grin.

I paused. "Troll…noses?"

"Candied."

"I…"

"And made of sugar and elderberries."

I laughed, then took one of the candies from the bag and popped it into my mouth. The sweet, fruity, and slightly acidic confection melted on my tongue. As it dissolved, I detected the spell woven into the confection… a lightness of spirit and a wisp of whimsy.

"It's delicious," I said. "And so very magical."

"Mother Urd, as we call her in Frostfjord, makes them. They are my favorite."

"She's very talented," I said simply, not wanting to reveal the magic of another maker. "Have you lived in Frostfjord all your life?"

At that, Bjorn shifted slightly. "Um, yes," he said, nodding as he chewed a bite of my farmer's pie.

It was then that I noticed the politeness of his table manners. For some reason, I had thought Rune elf halls to be rowdy places. Bjorn's manner was very refined.

"This is very delicious, by the way. I've never had anything like it before."

"Really?"

He nodded. "Elder Thornberry was right. You are very talented in the kitchen."

"See, your compass bird knew," I replied with a laugh, then asked, "And is your family in Frostfjord?"

"They are," he answered briefly, then turned back to the food.

"Do you have a big family?"

"Ah, yes…" he said, suddenly uneasy. He lifted his spoon to eat his soup, lowered it, lifted his tea to drink, and lowered it before taking a drink. Pausing, he stopped and reorganized his flatware.

Something about his family history was making him nervous, so I changed the subject. "So, how long have you been Master of Horse?"

"Oh, I…for…some time."

Another sticky topic? Why? "But you enjoy working with horses…and unicorns?"

"Oh, yes," he said, exhaling deeply with relief. "I spend as much time as I can riding. Our unicorns are unlike yours here, less elegant and more bedraggled, bulky, and rugged… A bit like Rune elves themselves."

I laughed. "I wouldn't call you bedraggled, but bulky and rugged…"

Bjorn smiled lightly. Were his cheeks warming red? "That's kind of you to say. After a few days on a ship, my beard certainly needs attention," he said, stroking his facial hair.

"I don't know," I said, giving him a warm smile. "I like it."

He gave me a grateful smile but looked away shyly.

"So," I said, clearing my throat. "The unicorns… Elder Thornberry has said there is something afoot with their magic."

He nodded. "I will visit the fields tomorrow and see what I can discover."

"I hope the elder doesn't have you camping," I said with a laugh.

"No, I think there's a cabin."

"Hmm," I said, then rose. "Let me bag you some scones for breakfast."

"You've already done so much. Please," he said.

"It's no problem. I'm happy to help, Bjorn," I said, giving him a warm—and what I hoped was inviting—smile.

But his reaction was…confusing.

A flash of some unclear emotion flickered across his face. He cleared his throat and turned back to his dish, fidgeting with the cutlery again. Seeming to realize his mistake, he righted his posture and said, "That's very kind of you. Thank you, Rosalyn."

Ugh, burnt ends! He has a girlfriend.
That has to be it.
There is another woman back home.
I need to find a way to ask him.

Turning so he wouldn't see the disappointed expression on my face, I pulled a basket of scones from a shelf. I set it on the counter, but I was so upended by the thought that he had a girlfriend that I bumped one of the vases sitting on the counter, causing it to topple over and roll toward Merry.

Merry, who had been engaged in a staring contest with Smoke, was surprised at the sudden clatter and presence of something unknown *hurtling* toward him. In typical caticorn fashion, he panicked and scramble-jumped to move out of the way.

That's when everything went wrong.

Desperate to escape before the *terrifying* flower vase got him, Merry's horn began to glow.

"Merry," I called, reaching for the vase before it fell.

And then, there was a blast of bright light and a popping sound.

Suddenly, every flower in every vase in the room levitated into the air.

Merry jumped away from the murderous vase and rushed to his favorite hiding spot behind the sacks of flour when he stopped cold and then sneezed. The effect was a cloud of glitter, and then, all the flowers in the room simply combusted, drifting apart into ethereal flower petals, their soft scents filling the room.

Bjorn, who had stood in confusion, watched as the flowers dissipated into nothing.

Merry shook himself, the little bell on his collar ringing, then changed course and disappeared into the back of the shop.

Smoke whined and went to stand beside Bjorn.

"Rosalyn," Bjorn said, looking about. "Is this...normal?"

"Being scared of ridiculous things? Yes. But this…" I said, gesturing around the room as the petals and aroma dissipated before reaching the tables. "Definitely not normal. Merry has been having these strange reactions the past few days. I thought maybe it was his allergies, but maybe not. His magic is upside down."

"Like the unicorns," Bjorn said.

I gasped lightly. "Yes. Just like that."

"Have you heard of any other animals in Moonshine Hollow being afflicted?"

"No. None. Only the unicorns."

Bjorn nodded. "And he recovers afterward?"

"Yes, he… Oh my gosh, you're covered in glitter." Hurrying around the counter, I brushed the glitter from Bjorn's shoulders, fluttering just a little to meet his height. I giggled. "You got more than you bargained for coming here tonight."

Bjorn chuckled, then looked at me.

Our gazes held one another's for a long moment.

Then, he quickly looked away and wrapped his hand around his forearm as if he were in pain.

"Are you all right?" I asked in alarm.

"Yes, it's just… I should probably get going."

"Of course. Let me finish bagging up some scones for you," I said, then returned behind the counter, confused.

"It's not necessary. I've given you enough trouble. What do I owe you for the dinner?" he asked, reaching into his coin pouch.

"Nothing, of course. It's my welcome gift to you, and my apology for all the…glitter."

"It really is no problem, Rosalyn. Let me help you with these at least," he said, reaching for the empty plates.

"No need," I replied, snapping my fingers. The plates lifted from the table and began floating toward the sink.

At least he liked my cooking, even if Merry's antics chased him away.

"I…I hope Merry is okay, and I do appreciate your gracious hospitality. You've been very kind. Thank you," he said, then gave me a polite bow.

Signaling to Smoke, he turned and went to the door.

"Good night, Rosalyn," he said, pausing as his hand rested on the handle. His voice sounded uncertain.

"See you soon," I replied, trying to sound chipper even though my stomach had formed into a knot of confusion.

With that, he turned and headed outside, leaving me wondering what had gone wrong. Was it Merry? Something I said? Something I did?

"Ugh." I exhaled deeply, sinking onto one of the stools at the counter. "I will never, ever be able to figure out men. Speaking of which, where are you, Merry? Your cloud of flowers just made my dreams of a fairy tale romance dissipate like smoke. I know you're a jealous boy, but really, Mer? Really?"

There was no reply from the cat.

Sighing again, I snapped my fingers, sending sparks around the room to extinguish the lights and lock the door.

"In the dark again, Rosalyn." I sighed and then headed upstairs. "Fitting end to the night. Come on, Merry. I have ice cream upstairs. Let's go drown our disappointment in sugar. Again."

CHAPTER 8

BJORN

"Just go to Moonshine Hollow and tell a little white lie. No big deal. No one will ever know. No harm done," I muttered to myself as I made my way back to Elder Thornberry's estate. "I'm going to help with the unicorns anyway. I'm not going there to socialize. I'm not going to meet anyone. It will just be a small bend of the truth. No one will get hurt. Right? Right?"

Smoke whined and looked up at me.

"If it's supposed to be so easy, why does lying to Rosalyn make me feel like I want to throw up?"

I exhaled heavily.

"I have no business getting close to her. If I can't tell her who I am, I should steer clear of her. I just don't get it. I lied to everyone I've met since leaving Frostfjord. It didn't matter until I met her. With her, it's different."

Different was an understatement.

Lying to her made my chest ache. With each passing lie,

I found it harder and harder to breathe. And then, when my runes began to glow in earnest… I had to get out. I had to go.

And I really *could not* go back because one thing was becoming abundantly clear. Lying to Rosalyn was not an option. It made me feel horrible in every way possible, whereas being near her made me feel…like *me*. I felt like *myself*. Sitting in her little bakery, listening to her talk, watching her work, her beautiful magic—and her beautiful body—had gripped me with an unseen force I couldn't understand. When she stood close to me, I smelled the sweet scent of vanilla clinging to her hair and skin. She smelled divine. She was so lovely. And she seemed to like *me*.

I shook my head.

"We can't go back, Smoke. It's not fair to her."

Smoke looked up at me, his expression questioning.

"Sorry, Bud. It has to be that way. I'll turn my focus onto the unicorns. That's why I'm here anyway. I'm finally away from everything. For the first time, I can see what I like to do, how I like to spend my time, where I like to go, like to eat…"

Memories of Rosalyn's delicious dishes came to my mind again, the soft, creamy flavor of the soup, the umami of the pie, and…her sweetness.

I sighed heavily. I hadn't come here for love. "The unicorns. That's my focus," I said again, trying to steel myself again. Trying and failing.

I had come to Moonshine Hollow to prove many things to myself. While I had lied about my identity to make that happen, the one thing I had not expected was to find someone so wonderful. Someone who only saw me as myself and was endlessly kind to me. No doubt, I had probably ruined her good opinion of me. My hasty retreat probably appeared rude at best and unkind at worst. I just… I couldn't lie to her anymore.

And my runes…

I was grateful when I finally arrived at the elder's door again. My head ached, and I didn't want to think anymore.

"Ah, Mister Runeson, right this way. The elder had a room readied for you. Do you need anything to eat? I'm afraid the elder and his wife eat early. Truth be told, Lady Petunia scolded him for not asking you to dinner," the woman said with a laugh. "I was sworn to ensure you joined the elder and his wife for breakfast."

"I would be honored," I said.

With that, the maid led me to a room that looked out on the vineyards and far-off pastures. Lights bobbed amongst the vines. At first, I thought it was fireflies, but then I realized it was fairies tending to the blossoms. Trails of light followed them as they zipped through the fields. In the Frozen Isles, it was too cold for such delicate creatures, but I occasionally saw the shy elementals in the forest.

Closing the curtains, I pulled off my clothes and slipped under the covers. With a tired sigh, I tried to get comfortable. Smoke found a spot at my feet and lay down to sleep.

When I closed my eyes, thoughts of Rosalyn danced through my mind. The softness of her skin, the smell of her hair, the magical glimmer of her wings. While there were many beautiful women at home, something about Rosalyn was special.

My mind replayed every interaction with her.

Her wide blue eyes, rosebud lips, and her sweet face. By the Nine Gods, she was so beautiful. She was curvy and enticing in every way. While there were always women like Ingri out there who wanted to push their assets at me, Rosalyn simply existed in her beautiful skin—soft, smooth, and so enticing.

I imagined sliding her dress up to her hips and leaning her back on the counter of her bakery. The mere thought sent a fierce throb of desire through my groin. I could almost taste her on my tongue. The sweet vanilla that perfumed her skin would surely mingle with a deeper, headier flavor that was all her just beneath. She would taste of honey and wild berries, intoxicating and addictive. My hand drifted beneath the sheets as I imagined her soft gasps filling the quiet bakery, the way her fingers would grip my shoulders, her wings fluttering as I kissed her neck, my lips trailing across her collarbone, down to her breasts.

My runes began to glow softly, a faint blue light peeking from beneath the covers. As my fantasy deepened, so did their radiance. Unable to stop myself, I wrapped my fingers around my already hard cock, the sensation drawing a low groan from my throat. My body reacted to thoughts of her with an intensity I'd never experienced before, as if it recognized what my mind refused to accept.

I stroked myself with slow, deliberate movements at first, savoring the building tension. My muscles coiled with need. I envisioned her breasts heaving, her body sweaty and trembling as she held on to me, her delicate pixie wings aflutter behind her. The image of her small body beneath mine, her eyes glazed with desire, her lips parted, made my cock throb painfully in my grip.

"Rosalyn," I whispered into the darkness, my voice rough with desire.

The runes along my arms pulsed brighter in response to her name, casting undulating blue shadows across the ceiling. My breathing grew ragged as I imagined sliding inside her, feeling her tight heat envelop me inch by inch. She was petite compared to my Rune elf body. The thought of her stretching to accommodate me, of her wetness easing my way, made my hand move faster, grip tighter.

Pleasure boiled within me, building toward release, yet each surge of ecstasy brought with it an equal measure of dread. Each fantasy of her body yielding to mine was both bliss and a frightening truth. The runes knew. My body knew. Only my stubborn mind kept denying what was becoming increasingly clear with each stroke, each labored breath, each pulse of light beneath my skin.

Our runes only lit up for the one we were meant to be with.

Her?

Was it her?

Every nerve ending in my body seemed to come alive, hypersensitive even to the sheets touching my skin. The mere thought of being with Rosalyn sent electric currents racing along my spine. My entire body tightened, my toes curling, back arching, breath catching. I imagined her voice in my ear, her breath warm against my neck, her nails digging into my back as she urged me deeper.

The runes blazed now, so bright I could see them through the sheets, illuminating the room with pulsating azure light. Each throb of my cock was matched by a surge of magic in my veins as if my very life force recognized her.

I pumped my hand faster, desperate now for release, imagining Rosalyn's legs wrapped around my waist, her core squeezing me. I'd fill her completely, make her mine in every way. The fantasy of her crying out my name as she came undone beneath me finally pushed me over the edge.

My climax hit me with the force of a tidal wave, wrenching a hoarse cry from my throat. My seed spilled hot over my hand as waves of pleasure crashed through me, more intense than anything I'd ever felt before. For those few precious seconds, I forgot about my lies and fears. There was only Rosalyn and this overwhelming need to be with her.

As the pleasure slowly ebbed, I lay panting in the dark, the runes still glowing, though dimmer now. Rosalyn was what I had been missing.

As I lay in the darkness, my heart still racing, the truth became undeniable. The runes recognized what my soul already knew.

But how?

How would this ever work?

She didn't know who I really was. I had been lying to her all along.

It was then that I knew with certainty that I had to stay away from her.

Being close to Rosalyn was far more dangerous than the lies I was telling. There was a very good chance this infatuation could turn into something more—at least for me. But I had started it with a lie. That was unfair. When she learned that I came with more baggage than a ship... She didn't deserve that. Or worse, once she found out who I really was, maybe that sweet charm would disappear, and she'd turn calculating. The idea that she might start seeing crowns and coins instead of *me* made me feel sick. I had to stay away from her...if I could.

THE SCENE AT THE BREAKFAST TABLE THE NEXT MORNING WAS both cozy and loud, but not in the same manner of our great hall. Elder Thornberry and his wife laughed heartily, joked loudly, and gossiped scandalously as they passed around bountiful platters of food. Their daughter, Emmalyn—whom I had met in the stables—was far more reserved than the boisterous pair. However, something about her energy reminded me of my sister Asa. Introverted, yes, but I detected a familiar spark of mischievousness behind the quiet smiles.

"My wife never let me hear the end of it," Elder Thornberry said as he handed me a heaping platter of fluffcakes, a fluffy, golden, and delicious breakfast pastry I'd never tried. "When she realized I'd forgotten to invite you for dinner, I thought I was doomed!"

"Oh, yes," his wife, Petunia, added with a wave of her teacup, the liquid sloshing onto the white tablecloth. "I'm so sorry, Mister Runeson. My husband gets so wrapped up in his business with the other elders that he forgets his name. I do hope you didn't go to bed hungry."

"Not at all," I said. "I grabbed a bite from town."

"Oh, yes. There are many fine establishments in Moonshine Hollow," Elder Thornberry began, launching into what sounded like an endless list of taverns, restaurants, and cafés.

"And where did you end up?" Lady Thornberry asked politely, though her eyes twinkled with curiosity.

I paused. "I... The Sconery. Rosalyn was kind enough to offer me a little supper," I said, trying to keep my tone neutral.

Emmalyn, who was mid-pour, paused with her teapot still aloft. Her gaze flicked to mine, narrowed ever so slightly, then softened into a knowing smile before returning her attention to her drink again.

I cleared my throat and looked away from her.

"Oh, yes. Poor dear Rosalyn," Lady Thornberry said, shaking her head. "Such a lovely girl. I can't believe she's still single. All the town's still talking about that terrible date she had the other night. The brutish man! Poor Rosalyn had to slip out through the kitchen to get away. A tragedy. Such a beauty and so kind and charming. It's a miracle she hasn't been snatched up yet! I even heard that—"

"Mother," Emmalyn interrupted gently, giving her mother a knowing look.

Lady Thornberry caught her daughter's meaning. "Yes, well. Rosalyn is quite the talented beauty and a great baker," she said, giving me an affirmative nod.

I turned back to my plate, avoiding Emmalyn's gaze. So, Rosalyn was unlucky in love. That realization twisted something in my chest. How did someone as beautiful and warm-hearted as her earn such a reputation? One more reason to leave her alone. If the truth ever came out that I was lying, I'd only be another mark on her long list of disappointments.

"Faelor will take you out to the fields this morning, Bjorn," Elder Thornberry said. "He knows the place well. We've already sent someone out to stock the cabin. You should be in good shape to stay a few days and spend some time with the unicorns. If you find yourself in need of anything, just send a message."

"Thank you, sir. That's very kind of you," I said.

I tried to finish up my breakfast without catching Emmalyn's eye again, but it soon became clear that the elder and his wife could spend all morning recounting local gossip, and the unicorns weren't going to wait.

"Father. Mother," Emmalyn said smoothly, "I believe Bjorn is finished, and it would do him good to get an early start. May I escort him to the stables?"

"Of course, of course! We don't want to hold you up," Elder Thornberry said. "Just remember to send word if you need anything. We all hope this unicorn issue is resolved quickly. It's got everyone in town on edge."

I rose and bowed politely to the elder and his wife, then turned to Emmalyn, who offered me a sly smile as she led me outside toward the stone-lined path to the stables.

"We'll see you have a horse to ride to the fields. And if you need anything while you're out there, you're free to ask," she said.

"Thank you," I replied, already sensing she was preparing an inquisition.

"What a coincidence," she said, her voice airy, "that you managed to find Rosalyn's shop after meeting her just that morning."

I reached into my pocket and pulled out the compass bird. "I have this little guy to thank. He's the one who led me to Rosalyn's door."

Emmalyn smiled. "Sometimes the simplest charms are the most honest. And while my father is right that there are many fine restaurants in Moonshine Hollow, there's no one quite like Rosalyn. Agreed?" she asked, a smirk already forming. I caught the same glimmer in her eye Asa often had. I knew better than to fall for it. So, instead, I leaned into it.

"It was a hearty dinner," I said with a perfectly straight face, "served with a warm smile. What more can a man ask for?"

I gave her the same knowing look I always gave Asa when I knew she was trying to bait me.

Emmalyn chuckled and let the conversation drop.

When we reached the stables, Emmalyn led me to a tall, golden-eyed man waiting beside a saddled horse.

"Bjorn, this is Faelor, our Master of Horse," Emmalyn said.

"Pleasure to meet you," Faelor said, politely bowing to me. His voice was smooth, deep, and laced with a melodic quality. He had swarthy skin, gold-colored hair, and curling horns. His goat-like hoofed legs stuck out from under his short trousers.

"You as well," I said, setting my hand on my waist and bowing politely. We had no satyrs in the Frozen Isles, so I was very pleased to meet him.

Faelor and I saddled up our horses, and we prepared the unicorn mare and foal to return with us to the fields.

"Be well, Bjorn," Emmalyn said. "I'm off to book club with some friends…and Rosalyn. I'll be sure to send your greetings," she said with a grin, then wandered off.

I shook my head and then prepared to ride out.

Soon, Faelor and I rode across the green fields to the far pastures where the unicorns grazed.

We were getting close when Faelor raised a hand to slow our pace. We dismounted, walked our horses to the crest of the hill, and looked out.

Faelor undid the lead on the mare, and she and her foal headed off.

Below us, nestled beside a glittering pond, was a small cabin. But beyond the cabin, a herd of about twenty unicorns roamed the field. The mare and her little one trotted to rejoin them.

I suppressed a gasp when I looked out on the scene.

The magic was wild.

Clouds like sparkling rainbows hovered over one patch

of the field. A dark cloud with glowing veins of lightning drifted ominously across another. A whirlwind, no higher than a man, spun across the grass. In one area, honeybloom violets—a favorite of all unicorns—stretched as far as the eye could see.

Sparks. Bolts. Whispers of incandescent glow. The whole field shimmered with energy.

"Can you cast protection enchantments, Mister Runeson?" Faelor asked.

"My mother never let me go far without at least one protection charm...or twelve. One of the benefits of an overprotective mother."

Faelor chuckled. "You're going to need them. This is the most magic I've seen stirred up in these fields. Be careful. There's a message box in the cabin. Send notes as needed. And don't worry, Elder Thornberry's homeland is enchanted. If you're badly hurt, the land itself will send an alarm. But let's hope it doesn't come to that."

"Indeed."

"I do hope you can solve this. We're all worried about what this might mean for Moonshine Hollow. If this spreads or begins to affect other magical folk..."

He didn't finish. He didn't have to. Moonshine Hollow was a magical place. If the illness spread beyond unicorns to people like him or Rosalyn...

"I will do my best. I swear it."

Beside me, Smoke barked at a sudden glimmer. Three phantom unicorns broke from the herd and charged toward us. My horse stamped and tossed his head nervously, but by the time the ethereal beasts reached us, they simply dissolved into glitter, whisked away by the wind.

I had my work cut out for me.

And for the first time, I honestly wondered if I knew enough.

Because if I didn't, this wouldn't be a magical retreat.

It was going to be a tragedy.

CHAPTER 9

ROSALYN

There was nothing I enjoyed more than book club. It was the highlight of every month, and I'd made the selection this month. I was a sucker for a romantic classic. While everyone knew the novel *Crown and Crumpets*, which featured haughty Lord Thornberry and the object of his affection *and* disdain, Miss Beth, whose family had grown to wealth from a thriving crumpet empire, it was my favorite book—ever. I was excited to have a chance to see what new perspectives the others brought.

Primrose, Emmalyn, Juniper, Tansy, Winifred, and I made our way up the creaky spiral staircase to the talking loft at Sir Reginald Hootington's Magical Bookery for our monthly book club gathering. Portia, the owner, was already there adjusting chairs. Sir Reginald's was one of my favorite spots in Moonshine Hollow. The loft sat by a tall window looking down on the street below. From the loft, we had a good view of the oak at the center of town. Patrons browsed books in the shop below us, many of the tomes wiggling with excitement as potential buyers passed. At the same time, an enchanted piano played softly in one corner. The place was serene.

Enchanted feather dusters cleared off our seats as Portia readied the place. Sparkles rose off the book spines on the shelves nearby, attempting to entice us to peruse the tomes. We settled into our favorite spots. Portia used her magic to distribute teacups, which clinked cheerfully as they hopped onto saucers. In the corner, nestled in a carved wooden box, was the shop's guardian owl, Sir Hootington, who dozed with one eye half-open. His midnight-blue feathers shifted, making flecks of silver on his wings glimmer like stars. A tiny wisp of blue smoke curled from his beak when he exhaled a soft snore.

Portia Wordsworth, our friend, and the bookstore owner, lifted her copy of *Crown and Crumpets*. Ever the sophisticated reader, her nose wrinkled as she looked at the book.

"Well," Primrose said, pulling her copy from a basket, "what did everyone think?"

"Loved it," Tansy, a newcomer to our group, said. "It's a classic love story. He was stiff, cold, and used to being on his own. She was loud and cheerful, just the remedy he needed."

I grinned at her, clinging to my well-worn copy of the novel.

"I agree," Primrose said. "I loved the subtlety of the romance. They detest one another for so long that it becomes obvious to everyone but them that they're madly in love," she said with a wistful sigh. "What did you think, Portia?"

"Well," Portia began, giving me an apologetic look.

I grinned at her. *I already know it's coming. Just say it.*

"I don't mean to be dismissive," Portia continued, "but I found it so…pedestrian."

The others laughed lightly. No one was surprised. Portia was a dear friend, but her taste in books always leaned toward heavier reads.

"At least we could understand it," Winifred told her, making the others chuckle. "I know you love him, Portia, but I could barely understand Bard Silas Drear's poems," she said, referring to our last read, which had been Portia's selection. "His ideas were lofty, but I could barely keep my eyes open."

"Bard Silas Drear is a master," Portia protested. "I had hoped you would enjoy his poems," she said with a defeated sigh.

"We did," Juniper said warmly. "The meaning was just a bit obscure, at times."

Sir Hootington opened one eye and let out an empathetic "hoo" before tucking his head back under his wing.

"I've heard Bard Drear's poems performed on the road," Tansy piped in. "When set to music, they *can* be very moving."

"Yes, I suppose so," Portia lamented.

"*Crown and Crumpets* does have its deeper meanings," Emmalyn said. "It's about being honest about what you want and truly knowing yourself. Lord Thornwick struggled with that, and I think that's a universal pain, right?" she asked tepidly, showing some of her own vulnerability for just a moment.

I nodded enthusiastically. "That's what grabbed me about this book when I first read it. I wanted to leave Spring Haven then, but pixies usually stay in pixie lands—at least, that's what my mother made me believe. But I knew I had to find myself. I also saw my own struggle in Lord Thornwick."

Emmalyn gave me a soft smile.

"And it *is* a spicy love story," Winifred said, fanning herself jokingly. "When he leaped into the river to save her, coming out soaking wet...whew."

The others laughed, even Portia.

I grinned. "There is that. And you all know my imagination is always primed for true love. I'm forever waiting for Lord Thornberry to sweep me off my feet."

"Would a Rune elf do instead?" Emmalyn asked with a smirk.

I paused and turned to her, a curious expression on my face.

Sir Hootington's head also swiveled in her direction, suddenly interested.

"Oh, yes," Winnie said, tossing aside her book with glee and leaning in to hear the gossip. "Let's talk about *him*! Who was that man lingering around your shop, Rosalyn? That Rune elf? What was he doing? Who is he?"

"He's working for my father and the other elders to help the unicorns," Emmalyn replied, gesturing to a sugar cube that did a little somersault into her tea. "He's staying with us."

"Hmm," Winnie mused suspiciously. "Well, he was practically stalking Rosalyn last night."

"I wouldn't call stopping by for dinner *stalking*," I replied. "We met at the elder's estate, and he stopped by the café for something to eat. He doesn't know anyone in town, and you all know I can't help but be friendly to strangers, especially the tall, handsome ones."

The others chuckled.

Sir Hootington hooted in agreement.

"He *was* lingering. I saw him at your door *twice*. You need to watch him, Rosalyn," Winifred warned. "We don't know anything about him," she said, then turned to Emmalyn. "Where did he come from?"

"He's King Ramr of Frostfjord's Master of Horse and a unicorn expert."

"Married?" Winifred asked.

"I don't know," Emmalyn replied.

"Girlfriend?" Winnie added.

I would have tried to stop her, but I was dying to know too.

"I'm not sure, Winnie."

"You didn't ask?"

"It didn't come up."

"And what manner of man is he?" Winifred asked, her gaze penetrating.

"Ladies, the book?" Portia said, trying and failing to redirect the conversation.

Emmalyn laughed. "I don't have your keen powers of

observation, Winifred. I guess… Well, he has good table manners."

I sighed, then sat back. "Unfortunately, all this talk isn't worth bothering with. Handsomeness and good table manners aside, I don't think he's interested in me," I said, remembering how Bjorn left hastily last night. I wasn't sure what had happened, exactly, only that something had suddenly caused his mood to change.

The little vase of flowers on our table sighed sadly, then drooped slightly.

"Shh, you," Winnie told the flowers, who perked up at her scolding.

"Are you sure about that?" Emmalyn asked me. "My mother mentioned you at breakfast, and Mister Runeson's cheeks were burning red."

"Sadly, yes. No angst-ridden yet sweeping romance for me," I said, lifting my book. "I don't know what went wrong. We were having an nice conversation, and then Merry had a little episode, and Bjorn left abruptly. He's no Lord Thornwick, I'm afraid."

Sir Hootington gave an empathetic hoot.

"Ladies, can we get back to—" Portia began, lifting the book, but Juniper set her hand on Portia's arm, gesturing for her to wait.

"Rosalyn, what happened to Merry?" Juniper asked.

I described the strange magical sneezes Merry had been having. Juniper leaned forward in her seat and listened, her brow furrowing.

"That sounds very similar to the issue Granik's new snufflecorn piglets have been having," Juniper said, referring to her orc bestie and a local farmer. "The piglets have been zipping around and leaving trails of truffles in their wake, not that anyone minds. Snufflecorn piglets are always wild, but this is strange magic. He asked me to come look at the fields. I didn't find anything odd, at least vegetation-wise, that might be causing it."

"Have you been to the unicorn fields?" Emmalyn asked her.

Juniper nodded. "I went with Kellen, but we saw nothing amiss. But the unicorns, Merry, and the snufflecorns…all magical horned creatures."

"Do you think there may be some connection?" I asked Juniper.

"There may be," Juniper said. "Is Mister Runeson still at your house, Emmalyn?"

"He headed out to Woodsong Cabin."

"He should be told," Juniper said, "don't you all think?" Juniper lifted her tea and sipped in an attempt to hide her plotting smile.

Everyone turned to me, grinning expectantly.

Even Sir Hootington swiveled his head my way, giving me a knowing blink.

"And you all think *I* should go tell him?" I asked, feeling a blush rise in my cheeks.

Everyone nodded, even Portia, who had pushed her glasses up to see me more clearly.

"Well, I c*ould* take him a basket of goodies. I mean, just to be friendly, right?"

"Of course," Primrose said. "Just like Miss Beth was friendly with Lord Thornwick in chapter twelve."

"And chapter twenty," Tansy added.

"And chapters thirty, thirty-two, and thirty-five," Winifred added with a giggle. "But especially chapter fifty-eight."

At that, the others laughed while Sir Hootington hooted.

I looked at Portia, giving her an apologetic smile.

"We'll see you next time, Rosalyn," she told me with a light grin "And in the words of Bard Drear, 'May fortune favor those bold of heart and reward them with love's purest art.'"

With a grin, I stashed my copy of *Crown and Crumpets* into my bag and hurried from the bookshop.

If Miss Beth could win her man through persistence, a well-executed waltz, and perfectly baked crumpets, maybe I could get Bjorn Runeson to warm up to me with a basket of scones and a smile.

Then we'd see what Bard Silas Drear would have to say about that.

CHAPTER 10
BJORN

Woodsong Cabin was a finely appointed space with a small bed, a table with two chairs, a stone fireplace, and a small kitchen. A glowing message box hung on the wall. The box was dwarven in design and shimmered green, enchanted by a witch or wizard. I'd never used one before, but as I understood it, you merely addressed your message to someone, wrote a note, slipped it into the box, and it delivered your message. Ingenious and curious magic.

Leaving my horse in the small pen attached to the cabin, I grabbed a few things from my satchel and headed into the fields.

As I went, I surveyed the landscape for any sign of disruption. I spotted no unusual vegetation, insects, or other features possibly causing chaos in the distance.

Pausing momentarily, I drew a rune in the air before me, whispering an enchantment for protection. I hadn't lied to Faelor. My mother, a gifted rune witch, had taught me rune magic. Protection spells had been first. The rune shimmered blue, bathing me with the protective spell. After casting the spell, I approached the unicorn herd.

The herd's stallion spotted me coming and stepped out to inspect me. He was a handsome creature with an ebony-colored coat and a silver mane and tale. His rump was dotted with starbursts of silver hair, giving him a celestial pattern. Amongst the unicorns, I noted a few other males with darker hair—deep blue, green, and purple. They, too, kept an eye on me. The female unicorns had smooth coats in every pastel shade and white. The mare that had been at the elder's stable and her foal grazed not far away.

I clicked to the stallion. "Hello, friend," I called but then began whispering an enchantment my father's real Master of Horse had taught me. Whenever around the animals, Master Runeson would evoke a calming spell, which I began to whisper now. I could see the spell take shape, a wave of runes floating gently toward the stallion, who watched me curiously as I approached. He breathed in deeply. He seemed to calm a little—but just a little. Suddenly remembering Emmalyn's gift, I reached into my pocket and pulled out the packet of sugar blossom cubes.

That did the trick.

The unicorn's stance relaxed. He exhaled deeply and made his way to me, sniffing curiously.

"So, Emmalyn was right. You all really do love these," I said, taking out a cube and offering my flat palm to the unicorn.

He took it delicately, his lips and whiskers dancing across my palm, leaving it slightly damp.

Once the others caught wind of what was happening, I soon found myself the friends of the entire herd...save those busy munching on the honeybloom violets.

As each came in close, taking a sweet and then wandering off back on their adventures, I looked them over. No sign of ailment. No runny noses, no gunk in the eyes, no outward signs of ailment.

But one young foal was running amuck across the field, his coat changing colors as he jumped and hopped, prancing around a kaleidoscope of butterflies. On the other side of the field, an old stallion was grazing, minding his own business, and farting clouds of sparkly rainbows.

From what I could see, the unicorns didn't seem to be bothered by the impact of the magic. Unicorn magic was always rather capricious anyway, making things beautiful, whimsical, fun...or smelly, in the case of the old stallion.

Only now, they seemed to have less control.

Across the field, a mare's horn lit up with a brilliant white light. She sneezed, stomping her foot, and a pile of hay appeared. It was so fresh and bright I could smell it on the breeze. The other unicorns joined in the feast.

I stood patting one of the young mares, giving her a sugar cube. Out of sheer curiosity, I popped one myself just to see what it tasted like—not bad, very sweet and floral. As the sweet taste melted on my tongue, I thought of Rosalyn again. My mind replayed her laughter, her easy way of being around people—something I was decidedly not so comfortable with, despite my mother's best efforts

—and her beauty. I had never seen anyone so beautiful in all my life.

The mare beside me snorted, shaking me from my thoughts.

"Right. You're right. I need to focus," I told her, giving her another sugar cube, then set off again.

I spent the afternoon scouring the fields looking for any sign of something in the environment, seen or unseen, affecting the unicorns. I studied their behavior and exchanges. Aside from their chaotic magic, nothing seemed amiss.

I also looked for any tell-tale signs of spells or wards that might be impacting them. It wasn't my specialty area, but I saw no sign of any malicious magic.

After an exhaustive search, I found nothing.

Unicorns were sensitive to magical changes.

Something *was* bothering them.

Maybe there was something else I could do.

I sat down on the carpet of honeybloom violets and closed my eyes. I was a Rune elf from far-off frozen lands, but magical blood flowed within me. As an elf, I was tied to the land, even if I was a long way from home. And I *was* royal. That gave me magical abilities that not everyone had. My personal magic granted me the ability to easily fix things. Could I use all my blessings to find the source of the unicorn's problem?

Exhaling deeply, I tried to focus. It had been years since anyone in the royal family had the deep and strong magical gifts of our ancients. Even rarer were the gifts of a seer. However, I often suspected that Asa's ability to get away with just about anything might have been due to more than just instincts. But still, I had to try. I closed my eyes, feeling the magic that flowed around me. The buzz of bees and the call of birds, not the sounds of waves and cracking ice, greeted me when I focused. I relished its softness. My thoughts got in the way when I tried to reach deeper. My mind drifted to a woman with flowing red hair who smelled of vanilla. Even as I thought of her, I could feel the runes on my arms warming. But I tried to push past that, to feel what the unicorns felt…

There was an odd bolt of energy, a strange shift.

Thunder rumbled in the distance, and I swore I *felt* lightning. Below the gentle hum of Moonshine Hollow was a wild magic. I could almost feel it, but it was just out of my reach.

But then, I felt something else.

A warm, glowing pink energy entered my space. As the magic drew closer, everything inside me felt soft, warm, and peaceful. It was such an odd sensation. It washed over me like unending waves of…

"Love," I whispered, then opened my eyes to find Rosalyn hovering before me.

Her blue wings held her aloft and cast a golden shimmer around her. In one hand, she held a picnic basket. In the other, I saw a very curious-looking caticorn with its head poking out of a wicker carrier.

She smiled at me, the warm gaze washing through me.

"Rosalyn," I said, surprised.

"Rose-and-strawberry scones, which are made with my top secret recipe, lemon-basil loaf, assorted meats and cheeses, and a bottle of bloomberry wine," she said with a smile, gesturing to her basket. "And, I think I might have an idea about your unicorn problem."

Smoke, who had been frolicking in the field with the unicorns, joined us, barking excitedly.

"And dog cookies," Rosalyn added with a laugh.

I rose and strode toward her.

Whatever energy this place held, it made Rosalyn light up. She was beautiful. Beyond beautiful. Perfect. Like the Lady of Spring herself. My heart pounded in my chest. I had met the love of my life. All I saw, all I wanted, was her. I strode across the grass, took the picnic basket from her hand, set it aside, pulled her close, and kissed her passionately. I melted into the softness of her lips, the sweet vanilla scent clinging to her hair, and the butter-soft feel of her skin.

I'm in love.

I'm in love with a total stranger.

And, as if to confirm my suspicions, my runes glowed bright blue in agreement.

CHAPTER 11

ROSALYN

The giggle that had bubbled up in my throat faded when Bjorn crossed the field with purpose, grabbed me, and put such a passionate kiss on my lips that it took my breath away. I saw stars, my head feeling light, and the rest of me feeling... My gods, how strong he was. He held me against him like I weighed nothing. His lips were so soft, his mouth tasting sweet from...was that sugar blossom? I breathed in his heady scents of sage, leather, and the ocean breezes that had clung to his hair and clothes from lands far away.

My stomach knotted, and deep within me, I felt bubbling desire. Warmth flooded between my legs, and a surge of want crashed over me as I pressed my breasts against him and kissed him back, only to feel guilty.

I had let myself take a moment I hadn't earned.

Giggling, I pulled back.

Bjorn looked at me with passion in his eyes. "Rosalyn, I lo—"

When he saw the expression on my face, his passion gave way to confusion. "Rosalyn?"

I took his arms and turned him around.

Behind me, the stallion that guarded the herd stood with a pale pink mare, their bodies pressed together, tails entwined, and horns touching. From their horns came an effervescent glow of pink, ethereal hearts and rose petals swirling in a potent love enchantment that had temporarily encapsulated Bjorn.

"I'd love to say it was my beauty that inspired you, but it looks like unicorn magic was involved."

Bjorn stared at the unicorns, then turned back to me, his cheeks burning red. "By the Nine Gods, I am so sorry, Rosalyn. I was thinking of you, and when you appeared, I just… I am so embarrassed. I don't know what to say. I'm so very sorry," he said with an awkward laugh. "That was so forward of me and—"

"No harm done—*at all*," I said with a grin, wishing my charms *had* overcome him. No such luck. "You are one hundred percent forgiven. It's a good thing you're a good kisser, or we may have had a different outcome," I said, then laughed. "You should see the expression on your face." I chuckled lightly and set my hand on his arm. "Really, Bjorn, it's okay."

He covered his mouth with his hand and then laughed at the absurdity of the moment. "If my mother…" he began, then seemed to catch himself. "I do apologize."

"Apology accepted. Please, forget it," I replied, wishing

with all my heart that he would *not* forget it. "Hungry?" I asked, gesturing to my picnic basket.

"I…" Bjorn said, seeming to realize he'd taken it from my hand and set it there when he moved to kiss me. "Yes, I am."

"That looks like a good spot," I added, pointing to a nearby willow tree. "Shall we?"

"You're so kind to think of me."

"Of course," I said gently, touching his arm.

One thing is sure, Mister Runeson. After that *kiss, I won't stop thinking of you any time soon!*

We made our way to the shady tree nearby. From there, we had a good view of the unicorns. Bjorn and I worked together, spreading the picnic blanket and setting out the food. I could tell by his actions that he was embarrassed by getting caught in the spell, and once more, I wondered if he had someone back home. But he'd mentioned his mother, which seemed…odd. Maybe Rune elves had some traditions with which I was not familiar.

Once the blanket was ready, Merry hopped out of the basket and selected the best spot, lying back down again.

"Will he run off?" Bjorn asked, eyeing the caticorn who was exchanging nose sniffs with the firewolf.

"Not Merry. He's my most loyal man. He never gets far, but mostly because he's perpetually lazy."

Bjorn and I both laughed.

I turned to Smoke. "I didn't forget you," I told him, pulling out a bag of dog cookies and tossing him one.

"You really are too kind to do this, Rosalyn. The elder left me supplies in the cabin. And I… I know I left abruptly last night. I am truly sorry for that." He paused and met my gaze. Behind his eyes, I saw warring emotions. "It wasn't anything you did. I'm sorry."

I took a scone from the basket and handed it to him. "Less apologies. More eating," I said, then sat back.

Bjorn gave me a warm and grateful smile, then settled in.

Bjorn Runeson was turning out to be a pleasant puzzle.

He set his scone aside and politely poured me a goblet of bloomberry wine before pouring one for himself and putting together a modest plate, which included the scone. But he lingered as he looked at the unicorns.

"Now that I've almost recovered over the embarrassment of kissing you without your permission, and my wits are slowly returning, you mentioned something about the unicorn problem?"

I nodded. "That's why I wanted to see you," I lied. I *totally* lied. "Last night, you saw the strange episode with Merry. He's been having odd bursts of magic. And then my friend, Juniper, mentioned a local farmer's snufflecorns have also exhibited odd behavior. Uni-horned creatures are most in tune with earth magic, aren't they? We wondered if maybe there was some connection."

Bjorn nodded. "You might be right. I don't know how it is for pixies, but for elves, we are also sensitive to shifts in earth magic. Something is wrong with the magic here. It's too wild, working in ways it should not. Look," Bjorn said, gesturing to the unicorns.

I scanned the field, seeing what he meant. Three colts chased a whirlwind of sugar blossom floss, a single rain-cloud poured over a particularly grumpy-looking unicorn, and sparks and rainbows shot everywhere. Everything was in chaos.

"Do you know these lands well?" Bjorn asked. "Is there any great source of magic out here, something that might amplify things?"

"I don't know. I moved to Moonshine Hollow to apprentice as a magical baker. I wasn't raised here. The ancient oak in town is magical. It is home to the fairies of Moonshine Hollow who tend to our flora and fauna. Still, most of the natural magical features are in Silver Vale, on the other side of the river. As far as I know, out here, there are just fields, vineyards, and farms."

Bjorn frowned, then sighed. He took a deep drink of the wine and ate a few bites from his plate. Once more, I noted the proper way in which he ate. Maybe that explained the comment about his mother. Did he have an overbearing mother who was a stickler for propriety and judgmental of girlfriends? Yikes.

Bjorn turned back to me. "So, you're not from here? Where were you born?"

"Spring Haven," I said, referring to one of the pixie home cities. "It is a small village, almost all pixies, and dreadfully dull. To be honest, I couldn't wait to leave."

"Your family…"

"Mother only. My father died when I was very young. I still visit her sometimes. And you? Is all of your family in Frostfjord?" I asked carefully. The last time I'd brought up his family, he'd hesitated.

"Oh…yes," he said with a hesitant smile. "Mother. Father. Three brothers and one sister."

"Big family. Are you close?"

"Too close," he said with a laugh. "Being here is like being able to breathe again."

I laughed. "I know exactly what you mean. Pixies have their own ways of doing things, and I just wanted to live somewhere with more variety of thoughts and ways of being. I love Moonshine Hollow."

"It is very different from Frostfjord as well. Everything here is more"—he paused and met my gaze—"charming." Bjorn cleaned his throat. "Frostfjord is loud, cold, and so constricting. Here," he said, then gestured to the fields. "It's all light and warmth," he added, looking back at me and giving me a soft smile.

In the distance, thunder rumbled once more.

Bjorn eyed the skyline. "Getting closer," he said, looking at the dark clouds on the horizon. He turned back to his food once more, smiling as he ate.

I loved watching him pick through the bites I'd chosen for him. He left nothing aside, trying everything with a smile.

"I'm sure you must miss something. Maybe your girlfriend?" I asked, trying to keep as nonchalant a tone as possible.

"No girlfriend. I love all my siblings, but my sister Asa is most on my mind." He turned and looked at Merry. "She made me promise I'd bring her back a caticorn kitten. Do you know of anyone who has them?"

"I do! Magnificent Meg, an ale witch who lives a bit

outside of town, has a pair that had a litter of kittens several weeks ago. I'll inquire with her. And also ask if her caticorns are having glitter sneezes."

"Thank you. I would hate to disappoint Asa."

The sky rumbled once more. This time, Bjorn frowned, then stood and gazed at the sky.

Smoke, who had been trying to catch the brightly colored poppy gophers who kept popping their heads out of their holes to tease the firewolf, whined and then trotted back to Bjorn.

"Rosalyn," Bjorn said, but he didn't need to say more.

Several of the unicorns were looking up at the sky. The storm clouds that had been in the far distance only moments ago were moving with haste toward us, the wind blowing. On it, I smelled rain.

"Oh no," I said, scooping Merry back up and putting him in his basket.

Bjorn moved quickly to help me gather my things. We had just put the last items into the picnic basket when the sky rumbled loudly, and thick clouds rolled in, letting loose their rain. At once, we found ourselves in a downpour.

"Come on," Bjorn said with a laugh, taking the picnic basket from my hand so I could carry Merry. "This way. To the cabin."

We hurried off, running across the field as the sky dumped buckets of water on us. In his basket, Merry meowed loudly in protest.

When the rain hit Smoke, his fur hissed, and plumes of steam rolled off him.

"I can't fly in the rain," I told Bjorn with a laugh. "And I'm a slow runner."

Bjorn chuckled and kept pace with me as we finally made our way to the cabin. Bjorn pushed the door open and we rushed inside. We were both soaked through. Laughing, with rain running down our faces, we turned and looked at one another.

Bjorn's blond hair was plastered to his head, water droplets clinging to his braids. The wet fabric of his tunic had gone nearly transparent from the downpour, revealing the faint blue glow of runes beneath the fabric. He was a sight to behold, even dripping wet. Maybe *especially* dripping wet.

While the spell that had ensnared Bjorn earlier was gone, whatever was trying to come to life between us hadn't disappeared. My laughter died on my lips as our eyes met, and that fluttering feeling returned to my belly, more insistent this time. No unicorn magic now. Now, it was just Bjorn and me, alone in a cabin with rain drumming on the roof.

"You're soaked," he said gently.

"So are you," I replied, not caring one bit about the water puddling at our feet.

Something changed in his expression. It was like a decision had been made, caution abandoned. The space between us felt charged with the same wild magic affecting the unicorns, but this was our own making.

Without thinking, I wrapped my arms around his neck and pulled him toward me, placing my lips on his. This time, there was no giggling, no pulling away, no explanations needed.

His strong arms circled my waist, drawing me closer.

Unlike the unicorn-induced kiss, this one started gentle but quickly blazed into something more desperate. He tasted like bloomberry wine, and once more, I caught that tantalizing smell of the ocean. My fingers tangled in his wet hair as his hands stroked my back, careful of my wings even in his urgency.

I melted into him, heat coursing through me. Bjorn met my passion without hesitation, his lips claiming mine with a hunger that sent sparks shooting from the tips of my wings. I pressed my body against him, feeling the hard planes of his chest against my softness, the pounding of his heart matching my own frantic rhythm.

When he deepened the kiss, a small sound escaped my throat—half sigh, half moan—and his arms tightened around me in response.

My head was spinning when we finally broke apart, both of us breathing hard. His blue eyes had gone dark with desire, and the runes on his arms glowed faintly beneath his wet sleeves.

Whatever this was, it was just beginning, and we were both lost in it.

CHAPTER 12

BJORN

I pulled back, breathing hard.

"Don't you dare apologize again," Rosalyn told me with a lopsided grin.

I gently touched her face. "I won't," I said, looking down at her. She liked me...*me*. Not *Prince* Bjorn, just my ridiculously awkward self.

Her wings fluttered, sending raindrops and a shimmer of glitter around us that caught in the dim light of the cabin. Outside, the rain pounded against the roof, creating a soothing rhythm that made the small space feel even more intimate.

"We're soaked," I said, stepping back reluctantly.

"To the bone," Rosalyn said with a laugh, wringing out her hair. "Oh, Merry," she said, letting the caticorn out of his basket.

Merry shook his fluffy white hair with annoyance.

Turning, Rosalyn cocked a brow and snapped her

fingers, sending blue sparks toward the stone fireplace. A moment later, a fire sprang to life.

"Works on bread ovens and fireplaces," she said with a grin.

Merry made his way to the rug before the fire and set about grooming himself, an annoyed expression on his face. Smoke joined him. Sensing the caticorn's dilemma, Smoke turned up the heat. His fur flashed red, drying himself and warming the cat, who eyed him suspiciously.

"Any clothes in this place?" Rosalyn asked.

"I have just my duffle with a few things, but Elder Thornberry said the cabin is stocked."

Rosalyn fluttered over to the trunk and opened it. "Hmm, let's see what we've got here." She pulled out a large woolen shirt and held it up against herself. It would fit her like a dress. "This will do for me. What about you?"

I couldn't help but smile at her easy manner. "I'll find something."

Rosalyn studied the shirt for a moment. "Alas, no wing holes," she added with a laugh. "I'll be right back." Winking at me, she disappeared behind a small changing screen in the corner. I went to my duffle and sorted through what little clothes I brought. Just a few changes of clothing and, out of habit, my royal suit. Frowning at it, I pushed it to the bottom of my bag and pulled out a pair of trousers and a clean tunic. I quickly changed out of my wet clothes, hanging them on hooks near the fireplace.

Smoke sighed heavily, sending a cloud of steam into the room, then lay down before the hearth with a contented sigh. Less damp but still displeased, Merry went to the windowsill to finish grooming while watching the rain with disdain.

Rosalyn emerged from behind the screen, swimming in the oversized shirt. Her red hair hung in damp waves around her shoulders. The shirt covered her to her mid-thigh. She'd pulled on a pair of green and white striped socks, which she found in the chest. They reached her knees. All in all, she looked utterly charming.

"What do you think?" she asked, twirling around. "High fashion. I look like a royal elf princess of the Bright Sidhe," she said with a laugh, referring to the luminous and reclusive elves of Aurelune.

I chuckled, the relevancy of her joke not lost on me. I gave her a warm smile. "The elder has excellent taste. I'm perfectly happy with that outfit," I said, unable to keep myself from flirting with her. Rosalyn was adorable, easy to talk to, and stunning. While I'd had my dalliances in the past, they were few and far between. A youthful summer love on Smoke Isle that ended in nothing. Another dalliance at the port when I traveled with the men. But aside from that, I had never really been in love. Infatuation? Yes. Sex? Yes. Love... No. And these days, with marriage foremost on my mother's mind, I dared not even look at a woman for fear of my mother inquiring about dowry and lineage. But Rosalyn was so...natural. I had never been close to a woman who had been so at ease in her skin *and* with me. Would she feel different if she knew I was *Prince* Bjorn?

She grinned. "As fashionable as this ensemble may be, pixies and rain do not go together. I need warmth."

I took her hand and led her to the fire, then got a blanket from the bed and set it on her shoulders.

"Thank you, Bjorn," she said softly. "Always so mannerly."

"My mother would be glad to hear you say so," I replied with a laugh, then went to the small kitchen area and prepared a kettle of tea, which I hung over the fire.

"Ah, the infamous mother," Rosalyn teased, her eyes wafting over the undone laces of my tunic and chest before she caught herself and directed her focus elsewhere. "Is she the one who taught you such impeccable manners?"

"Propriety is one of her chief concerns." I paused, feeling that gnawing ache in my stomach, the half-truth paining me. "What about your mother? Is she a baker, too?"

"Oh, not at all. She's a Butterfly Maiden."

I shook my head. "I don't know…"

"Butterfly Maidens are ambassadors of our pixie culture. They perform the silk dances, play the whisper-harp, and perform pixie petal potion ceremonies. She's a skilled singer, dancer, musician, and more… She was one of the most famous Butterfly Maidens in all of pixie lands. But she doesn't perform anymore. Now, she teaches young pixie girls the art."

"You didn't follow in her footsteps."

"Absolutely not. I was always in the kitchen."

"How did she take that news?"

Rosalyn laughed. "Your question tells me you've already guessed. She wanted me to be a Butterfly Maiden like her. 'Rosalyn, you are too poised to sweat over an oven. Rosalyn, you sing too well to waste time making cookies. Rosalyn, you dance too elegantly to be wiping off tables.'" Rosalyn gave a heavy sigh. "Eventually, she saw what my magic can do, so she let me pursue my own adventures. However, I think she always felt a bit disappointed. She greets visitors to our lands and teaches them about our pixie ways, and I... I bake scones in a distant city. We still talk, but I still sense some resentment."

"I'm so sorry," I said, taking her hand. And I truly was. I knew what it was like to disappoint a parent. Even though my father was only marginally interested in what his children were doing—he was content to let my mother do the parenting while he was busy attending to the kingdom—my mother was another matter entirely. Only Alvar ever managed to stay in her good graces.

Rosalyn sighed, then shrugged. "We don't live for our parents. We live for ourselves." She gave me a warm smile, and I could sense she knew her truth was not far from mine. But then, something in the clothing trunk caught her eye, and she hopped up to investigate. "Ooh, what's this?" She pulled out a small wooden box with intricate carvings. "Storm Stones! Have you ever played?"

"I don't think so."

"It's a game. Perfect for rainy nights like this," she said, bringing the box back to the fireside.

She opened the box to reveal a collection of smooth, polished stones in various colors.

"The rules are simple," she explained, setting up the game board. "Each stone has different powers and movements. The goal is to capture your opponent's moonstone."

She pointed to a stone tinged with white, blue, and a hint of gold. "But the fun part is that the stones have tiny enchantments. When you move them, they do…things."

"What kind of things?" I asked, intrigued.

"You'll see," she said with a mischievous smile. "I'll help you as we go. Are you up for a game?"

I nodded, settling across from her, Rosalyn arranging the board between us.

"I'll go easy on you since it's your first time," she teased.

My competitive spirit flared. "Don't you dare."

Rosalyn laughed. "Ooh, the Master of Horse has pride. I like it."

I chuckled.

She made the first move, sliding a blue stone forward. Immediately, a tiny wisp of mist rose from the stone, swirling in the air over the board, hiding the other pieces.

"Your turn," she said.

"But I can't see the stones."

"Exactly," she said with a laugh. "That's the fun. Either your stone's enchantment will break mine or mine will overpower yours. We shall see."

Moving blindly, I shifted a stone. The air above the board cleared a moment to reveal a green stone. A small sprout appeared from the stone, grew into a tiny flower, then wilted away.

"Pity, my fog blocked the sun. That stone is mine now." Rosalyn grinned, taking my green stone. The fog cleared from over the board, and Rosalyn made her next move.

As we played, each move brought new magical

surprises. Lightning crackled between stones, miniature rainbows arced across the board, and once, when Rosalyn captured one of my pieces—again—it let out a musical chime that hung in the air for several seconds.

I hadn't felt this relaxed in…well, possibly ever. Even with the real Master Runeson tending to the unicorns, I was still *Prince* Bjorn. The same thing was true when I was on my father's ships, even though the crew tried to make me feel otherwise. And with Asa, while we had fun, we were still royal siblings. But here, now… No royal duties, no one watching my every move, no need to maintain a princely demeanor. Just a game, a beautiful woman, and the rain outside creating a cocoon around our small sanctuary.

"Ha!" I exclaimed triumphantly when I captured one of her key pieces. The stone glowed bright orange with sunlight, pushing away her rain clouds before dimming again.

"Not bad for a beginner," she admitted, studying the board with narrowed eyes. "You're a natural strategist."

"My brother Magnus would laugh to hear you say that. He's the mastermind in our family. I spent my entire childhood losing to him in Frost Hnefatafl."

"Another game?"

"I nodded. Similar concept, different pieces."

"I'd like to try my hand at that someday," she said casually, giving me a soft smile.

At that moment, I felt both warmth and dread. The more she learned about my real life, the closer to the truth she would be.

Maybe if I just told her now... Rosalyn didn't seem like one to judge. She knew what parental pressure felt like. Perhaps she would understand. I opened my mouth and almost confessed everything, nearly telling her who I was, but fear held my tongue. What if she looked at me differently once she knew? What if the easy comfort between us disappeared? This moment was perfect. Maybe the most perfect moment I'd ever known. The truth could destroy it.

Rosalyn moved another piece, seemingly oblivious to my internal struggle. A tiny burst of colorful butterflies exploded from the stone, circling our heads before fading away.

"I have you now. Your move, Runeson," she said with a challenging smile.

I moved a red stone diagonally across the board.

Rosalyn frowned when a tiny bookworm, a small dragon known for keeping pests away from books, appeared and chased the butterflies from the board.

"Oh, burnt ends," she grumbled, then giggled when I took her stone.

"So, why Moonshine Hollow?" I asked her.

"Apprenticeship, originally," she said, her eyes on the gameboard. "I came to study under Master Baker Brambleberry, but then I fell in love with the town. The way everyone here is accepted for who they are, not what they are..." She captured another of my pieces. "In Spring Haven, I was my mother's daughter who was not following in her famous mother's footsteps. Here, I'm Rosalyn, baker extraordinaire and notorious romantic."

"Notorious, is it?" I asked, raising an eyebrow.

She laughed. "Ask anyone. Notorious and disastrous. But if the way this game is going is any indication, maybe my luck's about to change," she said, giving me a flirtatious smile. "Your move."

I glanced down at the board, trying to focus on the game rather than how her words made my heart race. I slid my stone forward, not entirely surprised when I realized too late it was a tactical error.

"Distracted?" she teased, swiftly capturing my piece. "My secret weapon works again."

"You have too many unfair advantages," I protested with a smirk.

"Is that so, Mister Runeson?"

"It is. All of which are very *distracting*."

Rosalyn lowered her lashes and then looked up at me with a warm smile. "Good."

The game continued, our conversation flowing as easily as the rainwater down the cabin's roof. She told me about her first cooking disasters as a baker's apprentice. I shared stories of the magical creatures I'd encountered in the frozen north. I carefully avoided the topics that might reveal too much, but there was an undeniable pull between us.

When she finally captured my moonstone, the game board briefly illuminated with a wash of silver light that bathed her face in an ethereal glow, sending illusory sparks of celebratory confetti upward.

"Victory!" she declared, throwing her arms up in triumph.

"Well played," I admitted. "Another round?"

She shook her head. "Let's save the rematch for later. It's getting very late. I should probably..." She glanced toward the door, but thunder interrupted her, followed by an even heavier downpour.

"You can't go out in that. The path back to town will be washed out by now."

Rosalyn bit her lip, looking torn. "I don't want to impose..."

"It's not an imposition," I assured her. "Please, stay. It would ease my mind to know you're safe. And Merry would never forgive you."

Merry, who was asleep on the windowsill, cocked an ear toward us but didn't open his eyes.

"If you're sure..."

"I'm sure."

Merry meowed from the windowsill as if adding his own opinion on the matter.

"See? Even Merry agrees," I said. "And I think we can trust his judgment."

"Well, if Merry says so," she replied with a soft laugh. "Thank you."

I nodded, suddenly acutely aware of the cabin's limited sleeping arrangements. There was only one bed.

"I'll take the floor," I said quickly. "There are plenty of blankets."

Rosalyn looked at the narrow bed, then back at me, hesitation clear in her eyes. "With the rain, it's far too cold for the floor, even with the fire."

"I've slept in worse conditions."

She seemed to debate something internally, then

straightened her shoulders. "Don't be ridiculous. The bed is small, but we can share it. I promise not to take advantage of you," she teased.

My heart hammered in my chest. "I... If you're comfortable with that."

"I am if you are."

The darkness outside made the cabin feel even smaller, more intimate.

We prepared for sleep in a dance of careful movements and avoided glances. I banked the fire to keep it burning through the night. Smoke, who seemed to have no interest in moving, stretched out as Merry carefully approached in search of a warmer place to sleep. Eventually, he curled up by the fire too.

When we could delay no longer, we approached the bed together. I felt absurdly nervous, more like an unsure teen rather than a grown man.

"Left or right?" she asked softly.

"Either is fine. You choose."

She slipped under the covers on the right side, and I cautiously joined her on the left, trying to keep a respectful distance in the narrow space. We lay side by side, staring at the ceiling, listening to the rain and breathing.

"Bjorn?" she whispered after a moment.

"Yes?"

"Thank you for today. For the game, the conversation… for everything."

I turned to look at her. In the dim light from the banked fire, her profile was soft, her expression open and unguarded.

"You're very welcome, Rosalyn," I said quietly. "More than you know."

She smiled, her eyes meeting mine. "Good night."

"Good night."

I closed my eyes, all too aware of her warmth beside me, the faint scent of vanilla that clung to her even after being drenched in rain, the whisper of her breathing. Sleep seemed impossible with her so close, yet I felt more at peace than I had in years.

Tomorrow, I would worry about unicorns and secrets and the inevitable complications of who I was. Tonight, I would simply be Bjorn, a man fortunate enough to share a small cabin and a warm bed with a woman who saw him for himself.

For the first time in all my memory.

CHAPTER 13
ROSALYN

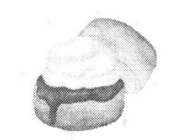

I'd never been afraid of storms, per se, but the storm raging outside felt different. In Spring Haven, my mother used to say that pixies were made of rainwater, pollen, and magic. Apparently, my father had some skill with weather charms, but that gift had bypassed me entirely. The weather outside felt wild and untamed, like the chaotic magic affecting the unicorns.

A deafening crack of lightning jolted me awake. The cabin shook with the force of it, and without thinking, I let out a startled squeak and pressed myself closer to Bjorn.

"Rosalyn?" His voice was thick with sleep, but his arm instinctively wrapped around me.

"Sorry," I whispered, embarrassed. "The lightning—"

Another crash interrupted me, this one accompanied by a flash of lightning so bright it illuminated the entire cabin for a breathless moment. The wind howled, rattling the windowpanes like an angry spirit demanding entrance.

"It's all right," Bjorn murmured, pulling me closer. "I've got you."

I looked up at him, his face shadowed but his eyes gleaming in the firelight. My heart fluttered, but not from fear this time.

"I've never heard a storm like this," I said softly.

"We get them in the Frozen Isles. Magic-infused storms," he replied, his thumb absently tracing circles on my arm. "They blow in from the sea, bringing ice and howling wind."

"Is this one magical, do you think? I don't remember a storm like this in Moonshine Hollow before."

He was quiet for a moment, considering. "Maybe. It came on so suddenly."

Our faces were inches apart. The thin barrier of space between us seemed to crackle with the same electric tension as the storm outside.

"Bjorn," I whispered, unsure what I wanted to say.

He didn't let me finish. His mouth found mine in the darkness, gentle at first, then with growing urgency as I responded. My hands slid to the back of his neck, gently pulling him closer. The oversized shirt I wore hiked up as I shifted, and his hand found my bare leg, his touch setting my skin ablaze.

"Is this okay?" he asked against my lips, his voice husky.

"More than okay," I breathed, my wings fluttering under the long shift with anticipation.

His hand traveled higher, and I gasped when his fingers found the sensitive skin of my inner thigh. I arched into his touch, my body already humming with desire.

"I want you," I whispered, feeling the words coming from my heart. This did not feel like my usual flirtations. Something different was happening here. I wanted Bjorn, but for more than just one night. I wanted him, all of him, heart and soul. "I have since the first moment I saw you," I confessed.

Bjorn groaned, the sound sending a delicious shiver down my spine. He pulled back just enough to tug his shirt off, revealing his muscled chest and the intricate blue runes that decorated his arms and torso. In the dim light, they seemed to pulse with a soft glow that matched the rhythm of his heartbeat.

I touched them with wandering fingers, tracing the patterns. "They're beautiful."

"They're reacting to you," he said in a tone of wonder. "They don't glow unless…"

I didn't have time to ask what he meant before his mouth was on mine again, more demanding this time. His hands pushed the borrowed shirt up further, and I helped him pull it over my head entirely, leaving me bare.

The cool air made my skin rise in gooseflesh, but Bjorn's gaze smoldered as he took me in, looking over my naked body. "You're perfect," he whispered, his hands stroking my soft belly. "Like ivory and roses," he whispered, then began to trail kisses down my neck, collarbone, and lower still.

When his mouth closed around my nipple, I cried out,

my back arching off the bed. My wings fluttered wildly, lifting me slightly.

"The advantages of a pixie lover," I said with a breathless laugh.

Bjorn looked up at me, a wicked glint in his eye. "Show me."

With a surge of confidence, I lay him gently on the bed. Straddling him, I let my wings work just enough to hover above him, my core brushing tantalizingly against the obvious bulge in his trousers.

"These need to go," I said, tugging at the fabric.

Bjorn lifted his hips, helping me slide the garment down his powerful thighs and off entirely. When he was fully nude before me, I couldn't help but stare appreciatively. He was magnificently built, all muscle and strength, and his arousal stood proud between us.

"Rosalyn," he said softly, a hint of uncertainty in his voice. He reached out and gently stroked my breasts, his fingers gently playing with my nipples. He paused and met my gaze. "You want *me*? Are you certain?"

"Yes. *Very* certain," I reassured him, lowering myself to press a searing kiss to his lips.

I trailed kisses down his chest, enjoying the way his muscles tensed under my touch. When I reached his navel, I looked up at him, making sure he was watching as I took his hard member in hand. His breath became quick.

"Rosalyn," he groaned as I stroked him, his hands gripping the sheets.

"Yes?" I asked innocently, my wings keeping me hovering just above him.

"Please," he whispered, his eyes pleading rather than commanding. "I need you. Please." He reached for me, his touch tentative despite his apparent desire.

I smiled at his endearing shyness and floated up to meet his lips for another kiss.

His hands roamed my body, finding every sensitive spot like he'd known me for years. When his fingers slipped between my thighs, finding me already slick with desire, I moaned into his mouth.

"Rosalyn," he whispered. "I want you."

"Yes," I groaned against his lips. "Yes."

That was all the encouragement he needed. Moving gently and with surprising strength, he lifted me as he stood from the bed, turning us so his back was against the cabin wall. My legs wrapped around his waist naturally, my wings fluttering to help support my weight.

"Is this okay?" he asked again, his eyes darkened with lust.

"Perfect. You're perfect," I assured him, already guiding him to my entrance.

When he pushed inside me, the stretch was exquisite, bordering on too much but exactly what I needed. I gasped, and a shimmering pink blush spread across my skin, starting at my chest and flowing outward like a blossoming flower.

"By the Nine Gods," he breathed, his forehead pressed against mine, eyes wide with wonder at the transformation of my skin. "You're so beautiful. You feel incredible."

For a moment, neither of us moved, savoring the sensation of our bodies joined so intimately. Then, with a roll of my hips, I urged him into motion. Bjorn didn't need further encouragement. He held me securely as he began to thrust, establishing a rhythm that had me seeing stars.

My wings worked instinctively, the magical glimmer from them bathing us both in a soft blue light that seemed to intensify where it met the glow of Bjorn's runes. Our bodies were illuminated by magic that responded to our passion.

"Bjorn," I moaned as he hit a particularly sensitive spot. "Right there."

He obeyed, holding my waist and helping bob me up and down, focusing his thrusts to make me cry out again and again. My hands on his shoulders, my wings working in tandem, I pumped hard, feeling my climax building.

"You're so good," I whispered. "You feel so amazing. Harder, Bjorn. I'm so close."

He quickened his thrusts.

"Bjorn," I cried out. "Oh, Bjorn." Reaching my pinnacle, waves of pleasure crashed over me. Bjorn held me through it, his movements never faltering even as I clenched around him.

When I came back to myself, I found him watching me with an expression of awe, his own release clearly not far off. With a mischievous smile, I whispered, "Let's go back to bed."

Understanding dawned in his eyes, and he carried me back to the bed, lying down without breaking our connection. I braced my hands on his chest, my wings spreading wide as I moved above him.

Using my wings to control my movements, I lifted

almost completely off him before sinking back down, setting a pace that had us both panting. The glittering pink blush on my skin intensified, pulsing with each wave of pleasure. My wings glowed brighter too, beating faster and leaving trails of shimmering dust in the air around us. The look of wonder on Bjorn's face was intoxicating. He'd clearly never experienced anything like this before, but truth be told, neither had I. It was magical. And for the first time, it truly felt like something beyond sex, something more, something…destined.

My wings beat faster as my pleasure built again, creating a vortex of magical energy around us. I tightened my inner muscles, squeezing him, and to my delight, the motion lifted us both several inches off the bed.

Bjorn's eyes widened in surprise before darkening with renewed hunger. His hands gripped my hips, guiding my movements as we hovered.

"Rosalyn," he groaned, his control clearly slipping.

"Give me all of you. I want you, Bjorn," I whispered.

That was all it took. With a deep moan, he found release, his hands clutching me to him as he pulsed inside me. The intensity of his climax caused spasms of pleasure to wash through me in a way I'd never experienced before. It was dreamlike. When I collapsed against his chest, my wings finally slowed and stilled, lowering us back onto the mattress.

We lay tangled together for several moments, catching our breath as the storm continued to rage outside. Bjorn's hand stroked my back lazily, careful of my sensitive wings.

"That was..." he began, seeming at a loss for words.

"Magical?" I suggested with a smile.

He laughed softly. "Definitely magical."

We stayed like that, exchanging lazy kisses and gentle touches as our bodies cooled. Eventually, Bjorn pulled the blanket over us and tucked me against his side, his arm around my shoulders.

"I never expected this when I came to Moonshine Hollow," he said quietly, his fingers playing with a strand of my hair.

I propped myself up on an elbow to look at him. "Expected what?"

He met my gaze, and there was something vulnerable in his eyes. "You. Us. This."

My heart swelled. "Well, I never expected a handsome Rune elf to ride into town and sweep me off my feet, either. Sometimes, the best magic is the unexpected kind."

Bjorn smiled, but there was a shadow behind his eyes that I couldn't quite read. Before I could ask about it, he pulled me in for another kiss, closed his eyes, and pressed his cheek against my head.

Nestled in his arms, I felt more content than I could remember being in a very long time. The steady rise and fall of his chest, the warmth of his skin against mine, and the way his arm held me close even as he drifted off to sleep all felt right. Safe. Like coming home to a place I'd never been before.

The storm outside quieted somewhat, though rain still pattered against the roof. Merry and Smoke had curled up beside one another, Merry playing the part of an opportunist and Smoke the unwitting bedwarmer. I saw Merry's tail twitching occasionally in his sleep, and I smiled. Even my fickle caticorn seemed at peace here.

I was just drifting back to sleep when I heard a faint, melodic humming coming from outside. At first, I thought it was just the wind through the trees, but the sound was too organized, too purposeful.

Carefully slipping from Bjorn's embrace, I pulled on the oversized shirt and padded to the window. The rain had slowed to a gentle drizzle, more mist than rain, and in the faint pre-dawn light, I could make out tiny points of brightness hovering near the edge of the fields.

Fairies. But not the kind that tended gardens in Moonshine Hollow. These were wild fairies, rare, royal, and notoriously mischievous. And they were…singing?

I watched, transfixed, as they seemed to troupe in a line toward the forest, carrying small lanterns as they went. This wasn't normal fairy behavior, especially not for wild fairies who usually kept away from human habitation.

"Bjorn," I called softly, turning back to the bed. "I'm so sorry to wake you, but you must see this."

He stirred, blinking at me in confusion before awareness returned. "Are you all right?"

"Yes," I said, my heart warming that his first thought was toward my comfort. "Come see."

"What is it?"

"Fairies. Wild ones. And they're acting strangely."

That got his attention. He rose from the bed, pulling on

his trousers before joining me at the window. His arm slipped around my waist naturally, as if we'd been doing this for years rather than hours.

"I've never seen them behave like this," I said, gesturing. "These are wild fairies. They never come this close to town. Should we… Maybe they know something about the magic."

Bjorn hesitated only a moment before nodding. "Let me get dressed."

We quickly donned our now-dry clothes and slipped out into the misty dawn, following the fairy procession. They trouped through the forest to a circle-shaped opening in the woods. There, we found a single standing stone covered in white flowers. The stone was ancient, carved in spiraling patterns that reminded me of Bjorn's runes.

Around the base of the stone, wildflowers were blooming, rare, magical varieties that I'd only ever seen in herbalist shops. Silver bellflowers, moon poppies, and the elusive starshatter lily, its petals changing color with each shift of the light, grew in abundance.

The fairies circled the stone, their song growing more urgent. As we watched, several broke from the formation and flew directly to us. One tiny fairy, no bigger than my finger, hovered before me, its delicate features pinched with concern.

"Pray thee, have you come to help us attend to our plight?" the male fairy asked, his voice like a tiny bell. "For the ancient veins of magic doth twist and writhe beneath the soil."

I blinked in surprise. Wild fairies rarely spoke to humans or other magical folk. "I…"

"Why hast thou come?" the female fairy asked, studying us. She turned to her male companion. "They doth be a pixie and a Rune elf. Make haste. Inform the queen."

The male fairy nodded, then zipped off, joining the others.

Bjorn looked at me, a confused expression on his face.

A moment later, a luminescent fairy with long, golden hair and shimmering green robes flew with two attendants toward us. She wore a tall, golden crown on her head.

When she approached, I curtsied.

Bjorn set his hand on his waist and gave her a short bow.

The fairy queen studied him, gave him a curtsy, then said, "Greetings, fair friends. Hast thou observed the odd magic about?"

"We have," Bjorn told her. "The unicorns are particularly afflicted. I've come to help."

The fairy queen nodded. "The magical balance hath been most grievously disturbed," she said, gesturing to the standing stone. "That which should be channeled through the stones has gone astray."

"Channeled through the stones?" I asked, confused.

"Aye, Mistress. The lines of magic in our realms doth require tending. This one hath been pulled from its course."

"Ley lines," Bjorn said softly. "The magical currents that run beneath the earth?"

"Indeed, Charmed elf," the fairy queen said. "As Midsummer approacheth, the sacred lines shift most unnaturally. We humbly implore thee to render aid. We have endeavored with our own magic to make the adjustments, but we are not strong enough."

"But how? How is the adjustment done?" I asked.

"The vessel needed lies before you," she replied, gesturing to the stone.

"We can use the stone to realign the magic?" Bjorn asked.

"It is possible, Charmed elf, but our efforts hath been in vain. We require *your* assistance," she said, gesturing to both of us. "A pixie and a Charmed elf."

Charmed elf? What did she mean? "Why us?" I asked.

"Observe, Mistress." The fairy pointed to me, then to Bjorn. Small flecks of magic flew from us to her hands, one an ice-blue sparkle and the other a vibrant pink sparkle. When she held them across from one another, they sparked, sending bolts of magic from one to the other. "'Tis the union of thy magics that holds the key," the fairy queen continued. "The magic of the North meets the warm and wild spirit of the Summerlands."

"Our magic together," Bjorn said quietly, glancing at me. "Pixie magic and Rune elf magic."

"But… But I'm just a baker. I'm not that powerful. I can bake enchanted scones and make teacups float, but this…" I said, gesturing to her hands. "This is big magic."

"Underestimate not thy gifts, gentle pixie," the fairy queen replied. "For 'tis not the volume of magic, but its nature that we require. Summer and winter magic doth the pair of you have. Together, it will restore balance. We leave the matter in your good hands and thank thee."

The fairy queen smiled, giving me a brief nod. "Mistress," she said then turned to Bjorn. "Charmed elf," she added, curtseying briefly to Bjorn before turning and fluttering back to her court.

My brow furrowed with confusion.

"You're right, Rosalyn. This *is* big magic. I know she is confident, but I'm not sure we can do this alone."

I nodded. "We'll need help."

"Kellen, the dryad, maybe? I can send him a message," Bjorn said.

"A message box can't reach him, but his fiancée, Tansy, can. She has a workshop above Thistle and Thyme, Juniper's herbalist shop. Help… My magic is for baking, but I know someone who *can* do big magic. There is a wizard in Moonshine Hollow. He will know what to do."

Bjorn nodded. "Okay, let's work together. I can go seek out the dryad."

"And I'll talk to the wizard. We can meet at Elder Thornberry's later."

The sun was awake now. A rosy pink light spread across the horizon, shading everything in a gold hue.

Having completed what work they could, the fairies zipped back into the shadows of the forest.

"Shall we?" Bjorn asked, gesturing back to the cottage.

I nodded.

As Bjorn and I walked back, I could feel his emotions stirring. Suddenly, he seemed tense and not because of the Ley lines.

"Rosalyn," he said as we reached the cabin, his voice oddly formal. "About last night—"

"Don't you dare apologize," I said softly, echoing my previous words.

He smiled, but the humor didn't quite reach his eyes. "I wasn't going to. I just... I need you to know that it meant something to me. *You* mean something to me."

Relief flooded through me but was quickly followed by concern at his serious tone. "But?"

"No but," he said, taking my hand. "Just... There are things about me you don't know. Things I need to sort through."

I studied his face, trying to read the struggle I saw there. "Whatever it is, Bjorn, you can tell me."

Oh, no. He's married. That has to be it. At the very least, he has a girlfriend. I'm a girl's girl. If that's the case, I will never forgive myself—or him. I'd never do that to another woman... Ugh!

Bjorn looked pained. "I want to. I will. Just not yet. Let's see to the Ley lines before something bad happens. The rest... Please just know, no one has ever made me feel seen the way you have. No one. Thank you, Rosalyn," he said, a sad tone in his voice.

Okay, so maybe not a girlfriend.

I didn't understand his meaning, but I nodded anyway. "I love being with you, Bjorn. Whatever it is, take the time you need."

The relief in his eyes was palpable. He pulled me close and set a tender kiss on my lips. I could feel the shift in his energy. His confidence was gone. Now, I sensed fear. He kissed me deeply, soaking me in, his kiss almost desperate, as if he feared it might be our last.

When we finally pulled back, he pressed his forehead against mine. "Rosalyn," he whispered, uttering my name like it was something precious. He gently touched my chin. "I'll see you soon."

"I'll find you," I assured him, trying to ignore the knot of worry forming in my stomach.

He nodded.

Slipping into the cabin, I gathered Merry, who was thoroughly unimpressed with being awake so early, and prepared for my journey back to Moonshine Hollow. As I left, I looked back to see Bjorn standing on the porch, watching me go. His expression was unreadable, but the slump of his shoulders spoke volumes.

Whatever secret he was keeping, it weighed on him heavily. *Charmed* elf. That was what the fairy queen had called him. Did that mean something I didn't understand? What was I missing? I sighed. Despite the magic we'd shared the previous night, I couldn't shake the feeling that when daylight came again, it might have swept away the connection we'd found in darkness.

As I spread my wings and lifted into the air, I made a silent promise—both to him and myself—that whatever stood between us, I wouldn't let it end our story.

After all, I was Rosalyn Hartwood, baker extraordinaire and notorious romantic.

And I didn't give up easily on the people who mattered to me.

And right now, no one mattered more to me than Bjorn Runeson.

A meow called from the basket hanging on the crook of my arm, as if Merry had read my thoughts and protested.

"And you, Merry. That goes without saying. Always you."

CHAPTER 14
BJORN

While the morning after the storm dawned clear and bright, I wished my thoughts were equally clear. Making my way into Moonshine Hollow, I couldn't stop replaying every moment of the night with Rosalyn—her touch, her laugh, the way her skin had glowed with that magical pink shimmer, her impressive use of her beautiful wings, the feeling of *rightness* that had settled over me when I held her.

But with the dawn came reality.

I had lied to her from the start.

Every smile, every shared confidence was tainted by my deception. And now, after what we'd shared...

Even the fairy queen knew I wasn't who I was pretending to be. In the Frozen Isles, our royalty was called "charmed." Rosalyn would not have known that, but the fairy queen did.

Smoke nudged my hand, sensing my distress. I scratched behind his ears absently.

"I know, boy. I've made a mess of things."

Sighing heavily, I made my way into town.

Moonshine Hollow bustled with morning activity. Vendors called out their wares, children chased each other through the streets, and the scent of freshly baked bread wafted from open windows. I kept my gaze firmly ahead. I needed to speak to the dryad about the ley lines. My personal issues needed to be set aside for now.

And I was more than glad to set them aside. I would have to tell Rosalyn the truth. And there was a very good possibility she would not forgive me.

The compass bird led me to the garden gate of a shop called Thistle and Thyme. A wooden sign decorated with herbs hung above the door, swinging gently in the breeze. The display window showcased glass jars filled with dried herbs, tinctures, and mysterious powders. In the garden, medicinal plants and flowers grew. I opened the gate and made my way to the building, which had a slight slant.

Taking a deep breath, I pushed open the door.

A bell tinkled softly, announcing my entrance.

The shop was a sensory marvel. Bundles of herbs hung from the rafters, their earthy scents mingling with the sweeter fragrances of oils and flower essences. Shelves lined the walls filled with neatly labeled jars and bottles. Behind a polished wooden counter stood a slender woman with long, curling blonde hair kept at bay under a handkerchief. She looked up as I entered, her eyes widening slightly, giving me a soft smile.

But her gentle smile was broken by a series of excited barks. A moment later, what could have been mistaken for a pile of moss scampered across the room to greet Smoke and me. Excited at the prospect of a playmate, Smoke leaned down on his front legs and wagged his tail.

"Pip is harmless, I promise," the woman, who I assumed to be Juniper, told me. "Are you Bjorn?"

"You know me?"

The woman smiled softly. "Rosalyn mentioned you… once or twice," she said, a twinkle in her eye. "I'm Juniper."

"It's a pleasure to meet you," I said with a slight bow. "I'm actually looking for Tansy. I need to speak with Kellen about an urgent matter."

"Of course," Juniper replied. She gestured to a narrow staircase at the side of the shop. "Tansy's in her workshop upstairs."

"Thank you," I said, then turned to Smoke. "Coming?" I asked him.

Juniper laughed lightly and gestured to the animals who were eyeing one another playfully. "There's no distracting them now. I'll keep an eye on him."

I gave her an appreciative smile. "Thank you. I won't be long," I said, then turned to Smoke. "Be good. There are too many glass jars here to handle a firewolf."

Smoke gave me a passing glance, then turned his attention to the mosspup once more.

As I climbed the stairs, I heard Juniper speaking softly to Smoke. There were two excited yips in reply to her promise of a treat.

The workshop upstairs was a bright, airy space with windows spanning the entire wall facing the street and the river beyond. An elven woman with dark hair stood at a workbench, carefully weaving what looked like copper wire through a complex arrangement of crystals.

"Just a moment," she said without looking up. "Almost got it…"

I waited quietly, watching as she made a final adjustment. A moment later, the entire piece began to glow with a soft, pulsating light.

"Perfect!" she exclaimed, finally turning to face me. "Oh! You must be Bjorn, Rosalyn's Rune elf. I'm Tansy." She wiped her hands on her leather apron then extended one to me. Her grip was firm, her smile open and friendly.

"I…"

Tansy chuckled. "Welcome to Moonshine Hollow, Bjorn."

"Thank you. Sorry to bother you, but I need to speak with Kellen. We may have a clue about the problem with the unicorns, but I would appreciate his perspective and help. Rosalyn said you would be able to reach him."

Tansy nodded, her expression turning more serious. "He's been concerned about the magical disturbances for weeks. I can summon him for you." She moved to a corner of the workshop where a small potted tree sat on a pedestal. Its trunk was no thicker than my wrist, but its branches spread wide, its leaves dancing with an almost sentient awareness.

Tansy whispered something to the tree, stroking its bark gently. The leaves rustled in response, though there was no breeze. She paused then and bent to listen, her eyes closed. After a moment, she pulled back and said, "He'll meet you at the arched stone bridge by the river in an hour. It's not far from the marketplace."

"Thank you," I said, genuinely grateful. "I appreciate your help."

Tansy studied me for a moment, her head tilted slightly. "Rune elf... There are only a few of us elves here in Moonshine Hollow. I forgot how we sometimes sense one another a bit *differently*."

She was right. With other elves, we could often feel their emotions and intentions more clearly than with other races. For instance, Tansy felt inquisitive but not distrusting.

"You're a Sylan?" I asked.

She nodded. "Newcomer to Moonshine Hollow myself. I was on the road with my caravan for years, but Moonshine Hollow—and its residents—called to me. It's a special place."

"It is," I replied, feeling her sincerity.

Tansy crossed her arms on her chest and gave me a thoughtful look. "You know, Rosalyn is a romantic. She flirts, charms, and makes everyone feel special, but she also guards her heart carefully."

I shifted under her scrutiny. "I'm not sure what—"

"I've known her long enough to recognize when she's truly interested in someone. And when she speaks of you, I see something that feels like...glimmer."

Glimmer. For us elves, that word had a special meaning.

"She's very special," I said, the guilt that had been gnawing at me all morning intensifying. "I don't want to hurt her."

"Then don't," Tansy said simply, as if it were the easiest thing in the world.

If only it were that simple. I gave her a soft smile. "By the Nine Gods, I swear I will do everything in my power to keep her from harm."

At that, Tansy gave me a genuine smile and nodded. "I believe you."

"Thank you," I said, then added, "I should get going."

Tansy nodded, then stepped back to her workbench. "Nice to meet you, Bjorn. If you need anything, one elf to another, I'm always happy to help."

"Thank you, Tansy."

She gave me a warm smile and then returned to her work.

Downstairs, I found Juniper mixing a pale blue liquid in a small vial while Smoke watched, fascinated.

"Everything okay?" she asked, looking up.

"Yes. Thank you for your help."

"Of course. You are welcome here any time," she told me, then turned to Smoke. "And you too. He's a very well-mannered boy."

"When he wants to be," I said with a laugh. "Thank you again."

She merely smiled, and then Smoke and I headed off.

As I went, I played Tansy's words in my mind. Something like a glimmer. That...was unexpected. But was it? My runes were whispering the same thing.

But the lie…

Gods, she would never forgive me.

I walked toward the river with my heart and mind spinning in a tempest.

Moonshine Hollow's marketplace was a kaleidoscope of color and sound. Stalls lined the cobblestone streets, vendors calling out their wares and customers haggling good-naturedly. I wandered among them, admiring hand-crafted goods, flowers, fruits, and foods. There was so much color, unlike Frostfjord's market.

I had stopped at a pet vendor, the man selling so many unusual creatures. In one crate were palm-sized fluffflehogs with petal-like fur that had a relaxing scent. Most were curled up into little balls and sleeping. They also had a pen of curdle mice, who were excellent at helping cheese-makers work in the making of cheese. I didn't know exactly how it worked, but even our cooks kept them. In another pen, I saw small foxes no larger than kittens. Three kits slept together in a heap.

"Sir, what are these?" I asked.

"Thimblefoxes," the jolly man replied. "They can find anything. Perfect for fetching lost items and sweet as candy floss in temperament."

I gave one of the little ones a scratch behind his ear, earning me a perfect fox smile.

"They're charming," I agreed.

"That they are, good sir. That they are."

"By the Nine Gods! Is that Prince Bjorn himself?"

My blood turned to ice. I turned slowly to find myself face to face with Chieftain Baldur, one of my father's oldest friends and advisors. The elder was always close with my family and seemed to favor me and Asa in particular. He had taught me to fish and hunt, and I had spent an entire summer on his island home on Glacier Isle. I could not believe it, but his massive frame and lengthy white beard were unmistakable, even here in the Summerlands.

"My prince!" he exclaimed, loud enough to draw curious glances from nearby shoppers. "What a pleasure to find you here!"

I forced a smile. Setting my hand on his back, I steered him away from the crowd. "Chieftain Baldur," I said quietly. "What a surprise."

"Indeed! When your father mentioned you'd traveled south, I never expected to cross paths with you. The king will be delighted to hear you're well."

I glanced around nervously, painfully aware of the curious onlookers. Among them, I spotted a familiar face— the gnomish woman with a shop beside Rosalyn. Her eyes narrowed suspiciously as she watched our exchange.

Had she heard?

What if she had heard?

If she told Rosalyn...

Oh, by the Nine Gods!

"Chieftain," I said urgently, "Please... I'm not here as *Prince* Bjorn. I'm traveling as Bjorn Runeson. I did not want to draw attention to my station, so I have not mentioned it to the good people here. I'd prefer they didn't know."

Understanding dawned in his clear, blue eyes. "Ah. I

see." He lowered his voice. "Forgive me, Bjorn. I spoke without thinking."

"It's all right," I said, relaxing slightly. "How could you have known? But I'd appreciate your discretion."

Baldur nodded gravely. "Of course. Might we speak somewhere more private? I sail soon but would love to hear what, exactly, my favorite son of Frostfjord is up to."

I nodded, relieved. Looking around, I gestured to a nearby tavern. "I must meet someone soon, but I have enough time for a drink…or three?"

Chieftain Baldur grinned. "Spoken like a true Rune elf. Let's go."

As we made our way to the tavern, I couldn't shake the feeling that we were being followed. Sure enough, when I glanced back, I saw a flower-bedecked hat ducking behind a cart. Winifred. This was getting more complicated by the minute.

The Briney Pint was a sturdy stone-and-stucco structure along the river. Inside, it was cool, dim, and smelled of ale. The place was busy, filled with travelers who had come in from the river. We found a table in a quiet corner, away from curious ears, and ordered two pints.

"So," Baldur said once we were settled with mugs of ale before us, "you've escaped the palace walls. Your father was less than specific, but I heard a rumor you jumped ship when a betrothal to a frost giant princess didn't go your way. Your mother must be beside herself."

I grimaced. "It didn't go *my mother's* way, which is partially why I jumped ship. I did leave a note."

Baldur laughed heartily. "Oh, aye, I'm sure that

comforted her greatly," he said, giving me a knowing look as he sipped his ale. "Ah, Summerlands ale tastes like strawberries and sunshine. Nothing in the world quite like it. I understand the need to get away, lad. The pressure of being a prince would weigh on anyone, but I'm not sure your mother will forgive you so easily."

"I couldn't take another day of it. With Alvar married and Magnus engaged, my mother threw every girl she could find before me. Some might think that was a good problem, but everyone I met only saw a prince. No one saw *me*. You and your wife are so well-suited, Chieftain. I just want a love like that."

"Ah," Baldur said, his eyes twinkling knowingly. "That I can understand. When I was a young man in my father's house, many women only cared that I was a chieftain's son. But Mara was different. She was my glimmer."

I nodded thoughtfully.

"And how has it been?" Baldur asked. "Have you found someone here who sees beyond all that?"

Heat crept up my neck. "Well, I…"

Baldur chuckled, clapped me on my back, polished off his ale, and waved for another round. "I've known you since you were no higher than my knee, Bjorn. You're a changed man. I see it in your eyes." He leaned forward. "Tell me about her."

"Well…" I began, and then, despite my reservations, I talked about Rosalyn—her warmth, kindness, and magic with food and people alike. "She treats me as a man, not a prince or a political pawn. Her smile makes me feel more alive than I've ever felt in the halls of Frostfjord."

"She sounds remarkable," Baldur said when I finally fell silent. "But she doesn't know who you really are?"

Finishing my ale, I exhaled deeply and then shook my head. "No," I admitted. "We've grown close, but if I tell her now, she'll think everything between us was a lie."

"Was it?"

"No. My feelings for her are probably the most real thing I've ever felt."

The halfling server brought our large tankards with a thud and an exhausted huff. When I moved to pay, Baldur waved me away and gave the girl some coin.

Pulling the drink toward him, he sipped, sighed contentedly, then said, "What will you do now?"

"I've made a mess of things. I didn't come here to fall in love. I just wanted to get away. Rosalyn deserves better than a liar."

"Then don't be one," Baldur said. "Tell her the truth."

"And what? Ask her to leave her home, business, and everyone she loves to come to Frostfjord? Ask her to deal with court politics and my mother's scrutiny? Ask her to give up her life for a man who lied to her from the start?" I shook my head. "It's too much."

"That, my boy," Baldur said gently, "is for her to decide. Not you."

I stared at him, his words sinking in.

"People are stronger than you give them credit for," he continued. "And love is more resilient than you imagine. But without honesty, it withers before it can truly bloom."

Before I could respond, a bell at the harbor rang out.

"That's my cue," Baldur said, rising. He polished off

the tankard and set it back down. "I wish I could stay longer, but my ship awaits." He clasped my shoulder firmly. "Think on what I've said, Bjorn. If you love this girl, tell her. And don't worry too much about your mother. Magnus's engagement was called off. Queen Maren may have forgotten all about you entirely in the dust-up."

"It has? Is Magnus all right?"

"Grinning from ear to ear, last I saw him."

I rose and pulled Baldur into an embrace. "Thank you, old friend."

"If you love her, have faith in her. Just...find a very good way to apologize."

"A good way to apologize?"

"Aye. Married folks spend a lot of time apologizing to one another. Best start off right and find the way that suits. Be well, my young friend. I shall see you again soon!"

He departed, leaving me with my thoughts and a half-empty mug of ale.

I sat there for some time, turning Baldur's advice over in my mind... *Tell her the truth and let her decide.* It sounded so simple, yet felt impossible. Her life was here. I had presented myself as someone I wasn't. Loving me came with complications. Even if she forgave the lie, it was too much to ask.

The tavern had begun to fill, and I realized I'd been there longer than intended. Kellen would arrive soon. Rising, I left a few coins on the table and headed outside.

The sun was high now, its warmth a welcome after the tavern's cool interior. I pulled out the compass bird, unfolding its delicate paper wings.

"Take me to the arched stone bridge to meet with the dryad, Kellen," I instructed.

The bird fluttered to life, rising a few inches before setting off down the street. I followed, weaving through the growing crowds. After several turns, the bird stopped, hovering before a narrow shop with a weathered sign reading Thorne's Arcanum.

I could see Rosalyn through the window, her vibrant hair unmistakable even from a distance. She gestured animatedly to an elderly man with a wild mane of silver hair, her expression earnest. The wizard nodded gravely, stroking his beard as he considered her words.

I stepped back into the shadow of a neighboring building, hoping she would not see me there. The compass bird fluttered impatiently.

"Very funny," I told it. "This is not the time. I need to meet with Kellen."

The bird circled once, then headed off in another direction. I followed, relief washing over me as we left the wizard's shop. The last thing I needed was to face Rosalyn before I'd sorted out my thoughts.

The bird led me through twisting lanes and across a small bridge, finally stopping before a familiar storefront. My heart sank. The Sconery and Teashop.

The bird fluttered insistently before the shop.

"My friend, I understand your meaning, but I must meet with Kellen first," I told the compass bird.

"Looking for something?" a sharp voice asked.

I nearly jumped out of my skin. Turning, I found

Winifred behind me, arms crossed, her expression thunderous beneath her enormous hat.

"Winifred," I stammered. "I was just—"

"Lurking," she finished for me. "Again. What game are you playing at, Mister Runeson? Or should I say, *Prince Bjorn*?"

My blood ran cold. "I don't know what you're talking about."

"Don't insult my intelligence," she snapped. "I heard that white-bearded giant clear as day. And I've seen you skulking around Rosalyn's shop more than once."

"I'm not skulking," I protested weakly. "The bird…" I said, gesturing. "I need to meet Kellen at the arched bridge along the river."

"It's that way…" Winifred snapped with annoyance, pointing.

I turned to go, but Winifred stepped into my path.

"Rosalyn is a precious girl, and she has been hurt before. Men who pretended to be something they weren't…men who lied. She doesn't need another heartbreak."

Guilt twisted like a knife in my gut. "I—"

"She deserves better than being lied to," Winifred continued sternly. "She deserves someone honest and true. If you're playing some game or just passing through looking for a dalliance, do the decent thing and leave her alone."

Each word was like a blow.

"It's not like that. I care about her."

"Then why hide who you are?"

"Because being a prince isn't who *I* am," I said, frustration bleeding into my voice. "It's a title, a responsibility, a burden—but it's not *me*. And it's all anyone *ever* sees."

Winifred studied me, her expression unreadable. "Rosalyn sees more than most," she said finally. "But you can't lie to her."

"And if I tell her the truth? What then? I'm still bound to Frostfjord. I can't offer her the life she deserves."

Winifred smiled knowingly. "How do you know what she wants? Have you asked her?"

Before I could respond, a tall figure approached from the direction of the river. From the branch-like horns sprouting from his head, I took him to be the dryad.

"Bjorn Runeson?" he called.

"I… Yes," I said, relieved for the interruption. "I'm sorry. I was just on my way, but the compass bird turned me around."

The bird cocked its head at me, as if to say "really?"

"You must excuse me," I told Winifred, terrified of what she might tell Rosalyn. "Winifred," I added, "please give me a moment to do the right thing. Please don't say anything to Rosalyn yet. I promise I will make it right."

Winifred gave me one last measuring look. "Tread carefully, *Mister* Runeson. Rosalyn has many friends in this town."

With that, she stalked off, disappearing back into her shop.

I joined Kellen.

"Is everything all right?" Kellen asked, his gaze going from Winifred to me.

"Just a misunderstanding," I said. "Everything will be all right."

"Very well."

"I need your help. Last night, I spoke with the fairies who live near the unicorn fields. They have a theory about what's causing the magical disruption. I need your guidance."

Kellen nodded. "The fairies? That's very curious. I'm happy to help."

"Thank you. Shall we go to Elder Thornberry's?"

Kellen inclined his head to me.

I cast one last glance toward The Sconery.

For Rosalyn's sake, I knew what I had to do. The right thing. The honorable thing. I had to let her go before I hurt her more. There was no future for us. I could never ask her to leave Moonshine Hollow, and there was no way my family would let me leave Frostfjord. This love was impossible. The thought broke my heart, but I hardened my resolve.

It was better if I made a clean break now rather than shatter her heart later.

I'd come to Moonshine Hollow seeking myself. Rosalyn…that was all she'd ever seen. Me. Just me. I'd carry that in my heart all the way home to Frostfjord. Once, a woman loved me for who I was. That thought would have to warm me the rest of my days, because in Frostfjord, the real me would be buried once more beneath the weight of my title and responsibilities.

At least Magnus had escaped a terrible fate.

For now.

I sighed. At the very least, I now knew I was lovable just as I was, even if this would be the only chance I ever had to feel such love.

Now, I had to put my feelings aside. My mother had taught me well. Princes put the good of the realm over everything else—even if that meant breaking my own heart.

I would do what I had to.

Even if that meant letting her go forever.

CHAPTER 15
ROSALYN

Wizard Thorne's shop smelled of ancient books, sulfur, something vaguely citrusy that I couldn't quite place, and burnt bread—which actually turned out to be exactly that, a problem for which my magic came in handy. With a snap of my fingers, I magicked the wizard's burnt cinnamon bun back to golden-brown perfection.

"Thank you, Rosalyn," the wizard said, stuffing a bite of his perfectly baked cinnamon roll into his mouth. "Ever the clever pixie."

"You're very welcome," I replied, making my way around the shop as the wizard hunted through his things. Every surface was covered with an assortment of magical odds and ends...crystals that hummed when you passed them, feathers that occasionally floated upward of their own accord, and jars of substances that seemed to shift colors when you looked their way.

The wizard himself was exactly what you'd expect. Wizard Thorne was tall and thin with a wild mane of silver hair that seemed to have a mind of its own. His beard was tucked into his belt, and small sparks occasionally danced through the silvery strands. His eyes, however, were kind behind his round spectacles, which had several additional magnifying lenses that could be swung into place for detailed work.

"The Ley lines, you say?" He peered at me over those spectacles. "Fascinating. And the wild fairies spoke to you directly? Most unusual."

I nodded, then perched on the only stool in his cluttered workspace that wasn't occupied by books or devices. "They said the lines were shifting unnaturally as Midsummer approaches."

"Hmm, that aligns with what I've been sensing." Thorne moved to a large cabinet and began rummaging through drawers. "The magical currents have felt discordant lately, like an instrument slightly out of tune."

Merry, who I'd brought along in his basket, peered out cautiously. His curiosity got the better of him, and he hopped onto the floor, sniffing a crystal ball that rolled away from him as if alive.

"Careful with your caticorn there," Thorne warned. "That crystal has a tendency to teleport people...and pets."

I scooped Merry up quickly and plunked him back into his basket. "Sorry about that."

"No harm done." The wizard pulled out a large roll of parchment and spread it across his workbench, weighing down the corners with unusual hunks of metals. "Now, let's see…"

The map was unlike any I'd seen before. Instead of roads and buildings, it showed Moonshine Hollow and the surrounding countryside crisscrossed with lines of magic.

"This is how they should look," he told me, gesturing to the map.

Then, he rolled out a similar map. On this map, the Ley lines pulsed with magical blue light. In some places, the lines curved and flowed smoothly. In others, particularly near the unicorn fields, they kinked and twisted unnaturally.

"This is a living map of how they look now."

"Look there," I said, pointing to the section of the map where the unicorns resided. A fragmented Ley line pulsed, vibrating wild strands extending to the farms outside of town and to Silver Vale, the magical forest on the other side of the river.

"Frayed," Wizard Thorne said, tracing his finger. "The anomaly starts near the standing stone the fairies showed you."

He pulled out a small wooden box to reveal two wands. "These are calibration wands. They can be used to help realign the lines. They are used during the realignment ritual."

"Ritual?" I asked, suddenly nervous. "Wizard Thorne, my magical abilities are pretty much limited to unburning cinnamon rolls."

"Nothing too complicated," Thorne assured me, "but it will require both northern and southern magic working in harmony. Your pixie magic and your Rune elf's northern magic should be the perfect combination."

"He's not *my* Rune elf," I said automatically, then felt my cheeks flush. After our night together, that wasn't entirely true anymore, was it? Or was it? Now, I wasn't so sure. Last night, I could have sworn Bjorn and I were at the start of something magical, but come morning, something had shifted between us. Had he gotten scared? I didn't know or understand.

Wizard Thorne, distracted by his thoughts, seemed not to hear me. He began gathering items and placing them in a leather satchel. "You'll need these maps, the calibration wands, and this"—he added a small glass vial filled with shimmering silver liquid—"essence of moonlight. It will help amplify the natural magic of the standing stone, giving you more oomph to pull the Ley lines back in place."

As he worked, my attention was drawn to a small orb on his desk that had begun to glow faintly green. Inside was what appeared to be liquid light that swirled in complex patterns.

"What's that?" I asked, pointing.

"Ah, a truth orb. Custom order for Elder Thornberry. He wants to keep it in his office to help him sort out liars. It detects when someone has been lied to."

"What do you mean?"

The wizard picked up the orb. "Lie to me," he instructed, giving me an amused grin.

"All right. Wizard Thorne, you keep a very tidy workshop."

The orb flared to life at that, bathing the workshop in green light.

The wizard chuckled. "*Touché*, dear Rosalyn."

"I know a charm for brooms and dusters if you ever want to learn it," I offered, making the wizard laugh.

He handed the orb to me. It suddenly flared to life, its light intensifying to an almost blinding brilliance. I nearly dropped it in surprise.

"My word!" Wizard Thorne said, quickly taking it back from me. The light dimmed considerably. "That's…unexpected."

My heart skipped a beat. "What does it mean?"

Thorne looked uncomfortable. "Well, it means someone has told you an enormous lie. Someone close to you, judging by the intensity."

The implications hit me like a physical blow. Most of my friends I'd known for years and knew them to be truthful. It could be only one person. I barely knew Bjorn, yet we'd become so close so quickly. And this morning, there had been that strange distance and a hesitation in his eyes. He said there was something he needed to tell me.

He's married.

That has to be it.

Ugh!

"It's probably just picking up on café gossip," I said, trying to sound casual. "You know how people can be."

Thorne didn't look convinced, but he nodded. "Perhaps." He finished packing the satchel and handed it to me. "The important thing now is addressing the Ley lines before the magical disruptions worsen."

I took the bag, trying to ignore the sinking feeling in my stomach. I had a mission to focus on. Whatever was going on with Bjorn would have to wait.

"Thank you, Wizard Thorne," I said, gathering Merry and the supplies. "I'll take these to Bjorn and Kellen right away." I fluttered to the old man, set my hand on his arm, and then gave him a peck on the cheek.

"Sweet girl," he said, chuckling lightly. "Good luck. And, Rosalyn, remember, sometimes people lie, not to hurt us, but because of their pain. Never assume."

I paused but didn't turn around. "Maybe, but that doesn't make it right."

"No," he agreed, "but it might make it forgivable."

With those words lingering in my mind, I stepped back into the sunlight, my heart feeling heavy.

TRYING TO PUSH MY WORRIES ASIDE, I WENT TO ELDER Thornberry's estate, where I found Kellen and Bjorn prepping to set off for the cabin.

They looked up as I approached, and something flickered in Bjorn's eyes—warmth quickly overshadowed by that same guarded expression I'd seen this morning.

"Rosalyn," Kellen greeted me warmly.

"Guardian," I replied, giving the keeper of Silver Vale a polite nod of respect. "Hello, Bjorn."

"Well met," he replied.

"You spoke with Wizard Thorne?" Kellen asked.

"I did." I held up the satchel. "He's given us maps and tools to perform a realignment."

Bjorn's eyes briefly met mine. "Thank you, Rosalyn," he said then turned back to Kellen. "I admit I'm relieved the unicorns are not sick, but this is magic with which I have little experience."

"What form does your magic take?" Kellen asked him.

"I can do many runic enchantments, but my strength lies in fixing things."

"Then I would say your magic is perfect for the occasion," Kellen replied, clapping Bjorn on the back.

I tried to get Bjorn to meet my gaze, but he wouldn't look at me. Was this the man who had held me so tenderly just hours ago? The one who had whispered my name as our bodies moved together?

Pushing aside my hurt, I opened the satchel and took out the maps of the Ley lines, spreading them on a garden table nearby. "According to Thorne, the disruption is centered near the standing stone. These twisted sections are affecting the unicorn fields, and the fraying is impacting other areas where horned magical creatures, like Merry and the snufflecorns, live."

Kellen leaned in, studying the map with interest. "This explains why my connection to the forest has felt strained. The Ley lines run through Silver Vale as well, and the residents of my forest have been more mischievous than usual. Something has them irritated. This makes sense."

Bjorn stood with his arms crossed on his chest. His eyes were focused on the map. "The fairies mentioned a ritual to realign the currents. Did Thorne explain how that works?"

"He gave us these calibration wands," I said, opening the wooden box. "And this should amplify the stone's natural magic," I said, gesturing to the potion he'd given me.

"And the realignment itself?" Kellen asked.

"That's where it gets complicated. Thorne says it requires both northern and southern magic working together." I glanced at Bjorn. "Luckily, he mentioned that Rune elf and pixie magic will work. Our magic can pull the Ley lines when we use the wands."

Bjorn nodded slowly. "Very well. Let's work together."

I studied him for a moment. "I'd like nothing more."

Bjorn smiled softly, but there was a sadness in his gaze I didn't understand.

Kellen looked between us, clearly sensing the tension. "Perhaps we should consult with Elder Thornberry before proceeding," he said, gesturing to the house.

"Good idea," Bjorn said, relieved at the subject change.

I collected the supplies and slipped them back into the satchel. "Lead the way," I said simply, but my heart thumped in my chest.

Whatever Bjorn needed time to consider was now weighing heavily on him.

I felt its denseness deep within me.

And to my great despair, it felt like the end to something that had barely begun to bloom.

Elder Thornberry welcomed us into his study, a cozy room lined with bookshelves and dominated by a large desk covered in papers and small magical artifacts. Maps and diagrams covered one wall, while another featured a collection of embroidery circles, all made by his wife.

"Ley lines, eh?" The elder stroked his beard thoughtfully after we explained the situation. "Now, that makes sense. I think I have something for you." He moved to a bookshelf, pulling down a heavy tome bound in weathered leather. "I remember a story… There was a similar disruption in Moonshine Hollow many, many years ago. I only remember it because my great-grandfather wrote about how rainbows filled the sky. His description was gripping and never left my imagination. It's in the family chronicles."

As he leafed through the yellowed pages, I stole glances at Bjorn. He stood by the window, the sunlight catching in his golden hair. His profile was so perfect it almost hurt to look at him. Last night, I'd traced those features with my fingertips, memorizing every line and plane by touch as much as sight.

Now, he felt a world away.

"Ah, here it is!" Elder Thornberry exclaimed, pulling me from my thoughts. "They called it the Great Divergence. Flashy name, isn't it? The Ley lines shifted dramatically that year, causing all manner of magical chaos."

He turned the book so we could see an illustration depicting a scene remarkably similar to what we'd witnessed in the unicorn fields. There were magical creatures surrounded by chaotic bursts of uncontrolled power and rainbows filling the sky overhead.

"How did they fix it?" Kellen asked. "Did they use calibration wands as the wizard suggested?"

The elder turned the page to reveal a drawing of a perfect circle of stone with an opening at the center. There were intricate spiral patterns carved into its surface. "Ah-ha! They used the Thread Stone. The fairies were right that the stones were the key. The Thread Stone acts as a... Well, think of it as the eye of a needle. Thread the Ley lines through, and *voilà*!"

"Where is this stone?" Bjorn asked, moving closer.

"Deep in the Whispering Woods, not far from where you met the fairies," Elder Thornberry said. "It's been largely forgotten. Few have need of such old magic these days."

"Seems like we need it now," I said.

The elder nodded. "Indeed we do, dear Rosalyn. And we'll need to work quickly. According to this," he said, tapping the tome, "if the lines remain disrupted through Midsummer, the magical disturbances could become permanent."

Bjorn and Kellen exchanged looks.

"We should make ready to head out immediately," Kellen said. "This is deep in the forest."

Bjorn nodded. "Thank you, Elder Thornberry. We appreciate your assistance."

"I need to attend to something," I told Kellen. "I'll meet you outside in fifteen minutes or so?"

The dryad nodded.

Bjorn, however, did not meet my gaze.

As the men continued discussing logistics, I slipped away to beseech Emmalyn's help.

I found her in the stables, grooming a beautiful chestnut mare. She looked up as I entered, her face breaking into a warm smile.

"Rosalyn! What a lovely surprise." She set down her brush and dusted off her hands. "Come to brighten my day with baked goods?"

"Not exactly," I said, trying to smile but not quite managing it. "I'm headed out with Kellen and Bjorn to Whispering Woods. I wondered if you would mind going by the shop to let Zarina know I might be detained for a while?"

"Of course. The Whispering Woods?" Her eyebrows rose. "What business do you have there? Those woods are not for casual wandering."

"We think we've discovered the source of the chaotic magic. It's a long story involving unicorns, wild fairies, and magical disruptions." I leaned against a stall door, suddenly feeling exhausted. "And apparently, a stone circle that can fix it all."

"Hmm," Emmalyn mused, then looked me over. "I'll see to Zarina, but what's really bothering you? You look like you accidentally used salt instead of sugar in a birthday cake."

I hesitated, but the concern in her eyes broke through

my defenses. "It's Bjorn," I admitted. "We had a moment… A rare, magical night, but this morning, something changed. He's pulled away, and I don't understand why."

"Men are strange creatures."

"It's more than that. Wizard Thorne had an orb that detects lies, and when it came near me, it lit up like a Midsummer bonfire. And now I can't stop wondering—"

"If Bjorn lied to you," Emmalyn finished for me.

I nodded miserably. "And about what? He's built a wall between us, and I don't know why."

Emmalyn was quiet momentarily, then said, "Some secrets are hard to share, especially when you're afraid of how the other person might react."

"But after what happened between us…" I broke off, not wanting to be too explicit about our night together.

"Lord Thornwick level?"

"And then some."

Emmalyn sighed softly. "Vulnerability can be terrifying."

I sighed. "I just wish he'd talk to me. Whatever it is, we could work through it together."

"Have you told him that?"

"I haven't had the chance. He's barely looked at me today."

"Rosalyn, I've known you since you came to Moonshine Hollow. You've never been one to sit back and wait for things to happen. Talk to him."

"And if he has a girlfriend? Or worse…"

"Better to know than wonder."

I managed a small smile. "You're right. Once this

Thread Stone business is sorted out, I'm going to corner that Rune elf and get the truth, whatever it is."

"That's the Rosalyn I know," Emmalyn said with a grin.

I hugged her.

"I smell like horses," Emmalyn said.

"I love you just as you are."

"Horse smell and all?"

"Of course."

We pulled back.

"I'll wash up and head to your shop," Emmalyn told me. "I've been craving chocolate chip muffins all morning anyway."

"Thank you."

"Anything, friend. And good luck. Something tells me that Bjorn is a good man. Have faith."

"I'll try."

As I went, I sighed heavily. No matter how distant Bjorn was today, I couldn't forget how he'd held me last night or how his runes glowed when we touched. He was keeping something from me. That was clear. But what we had together? That hadn't been a lie. That had been real.

And I wasn't ready to give up on real just yet.

CHAPTER 16
BJORN

The Whispering Woods lived up to its name. As we made our way through the ancient trees, their leaves rustled with soft murmurs that almost sounded like words. Smoke padded silently at my side, occasionally sniffing the air with wary interest, while Merry rode in Rosalyn's basket, his little golden horn peeking out as he surveyed our surroundings.

I walked a few paces behind Rosalyn and Kellen, watching as sunlight filtered through the canopy above, creating dancing patterns on Rosalyn's wings and hair. She was so easy with people, and her nature was so kind. Perhaps she hadn't followed her mother's path to becoming an ambassador of her culture, but I saw how her presence softened all around her. Even the stoic dryad smiled and eased in her presence. Every time she laughed at something Kellen said, something twisted painfully in my chest. I should be the one making her laugh, not maintaining this careful distance.

The truth of my situation was inescapable. Now that Winifred had learned my secret, everything was ruined. That brief dream, that I was simply a man loved by a woman, was over as quickly as it had come to life. Once more, I was Prince Bjorn of Frostfjord, heir to duty and responsibility. And she was Rosalyn Hartwood of Moonshine Hollow, whose life and business were firmly rooted here in the Summerlands.

To let myself love her—or to let her love me—would only lead to heartbreak for both of us.

And yet, I couldn't look away from her.

"We're getting close," Kellen said. "I can feel the forest's energy shifting."

Rosalyn nodded, her wings fluttering slightly. "Something here feels…ancient."

She wasn't wrong. The deeper we ventured into the woods, the more I felt a strange resonance with the land. It reminded me of the sacred groves back home. My runes tingled beneath my skin, responding to the magic in the air.

"Do you feel that?" I asked without thinking.

Rosalyn glanced back at me, a questioning look in her eyes. "Yes," she said softly. "It's like the air is…singing."

Our eyes held for a moment too long before I forced myself to look away. "It feels similar to old places in Frostfjord," I said, fighting to keep my voice neutral.

"Your homeland must be beautiful," Rosalyn said, an edge of something—Hurt? Curiosity?—in her voice.

"It is a stark beauty."

"I have visited Dryad Aelderin on Brunndale before. It is a rugged place. As for me, I prefer places that don't freeze your bones," Kellen interjected with a chuckle, breaking the tension. "While my connection is closest with Silver Vale, the forest here still whispers. Its voice is ancient and quiet, but I believe we've found what we're looking for."

The trees opened into a small clearing, revealing the Thread Stone. Unlike the standing stone the fairies had shown us, this was a perfect circle of pale gray stone about waist-high, with an opening in the center large enough to pass an arm through. Intricate carvings spiraled across its surface, some resembling runes that were not unlike those that marked my skin. Moss and violets grew at its base.

"Wow, it's beautiful," Rosalyn whispered.

I found myself nodding in agreement. "And powerful."

Kellen approached it cautiously. "No wonder the fairies couldn't fix this themselves. This kind of old magic requires something different to channel it." He glanced back at us. "Sometimes they say things are meant to be. What are the chances we'd have a Rune elf and a pixie in Moonshine Hollow at the same time? Your magic creates a duality. This *should* work."

Setting down his pack, Kellen began clearing the area around the stone of debris and fallen leaves. Rosalyn helped, placing Merry's basket in a safe spot before joining the dryad.

I hesitated a moment, then pulled out the map of the Ley lines. "So, we must pull the frayed lines back and rethread them through the stone. Once we do, they should continue on to the standing stone where Rosalyn and I met the fairies, and from then on, be in alignment."

"Can this stone really fix all that?" Rosalyn asked, eyeing the Thread Stone skeptically.

"The calibration wands should help us direct the energy where it needs to go," I replied.

Kellen gave the stone a pensive look. "It's going to take considerable power. Are you both prepared for that?"

Rosalyn and I exchanged glances.

"What do you mean by considerable?" she asked, a worried expression on her face.

"Based on what I understand from Elder Thornberry's book, you'll need to channel your magic through the stone, with Bjorn acting as the northern pole on one side and you acting on the southern pole on the other. Bjorn will refocus the magic into a straight line, but you must use your magnetism to pull it through," Kellen explained. "It will be like redirecting a river with your bare hands. I will do what I can to ground the energy with earth magic, to steady it, but you should expect… It will be a lot."

Rosalyn paused, then looked at me. "If we work together, Bjorn and I can handle it."

My heart skipped a beat at her words, which were clearly about more than the Ley lines. I gave her a soft smile, chiding myself for my distance toward her and any hurt it may have caused her.

"Good. Let's prepare," Kellen said.

We spent the next hour getting ready. Kellen gathered specific plants and herbs to help stabilize the ritual, arranging them in a circular pattern around the Thread Stone. I examined the stone more closely, studying its runes. Many were familiar, symbols for balance, harmony, and connection, but others were unlike any I'd encountered. If I cast enchantments similar to those on the stone, it may help me pull the Ley lines back in place to thread them through to Rosalyn.

Rosalyn, meanwhile, prepared the calibration wands and the vial of moonlight essence. She handled the magical tools with surprising deftness for someone who claimed to have limited magical abilities. Perhaps she was underestimating her skills.

Finally, Kellen nodded, satisfied with his work.

"I think I'm ready. You two?"

Rosalyn and I both nodded.

"Bjorn, you should stand there." He pointed to one side of the Thread Stone. "And, Rosalyn, you there." He indicated the opposite side. "I'll ground the magic as best I can and maintain a protection barrier around us. This kind of magic can have…unpredictable effects."

We took our positions. Rosalyn looked at me across the stone circle, her blue eyes reflecting the now-dying sunlight.

"Ready?" she asked softly.

"Ready."

Kellen handed us each a calibration wand. "Visualize the lines straightening and flowing properly."

Rosalyn uncorked the vial of moonlight essence and carefully poured it over the Thread Stone. The liquid seemed to sink into the stone, causing the carved runes to glow with a soft silver light.

I nodded to her and began casting myself, drawing enchantments for the runes in the air. As I did so, the air around us began to feel charged. The hair on my arms rose, and I heard the crackle of magic.

"It's reacting already, Bjorn," Kellen said excitedly.

"The runic enchantments will help strengthen my pull," I replied.

"Bjorn," Kellen said, "don't forget. You fix things. That's what you do. You can do this. Rosalyn?"

"I'm ready," she said, raising her wand.

"Welcome the energy to the south," Kellen told her. "Call it forth with all your pixie tenderness and warmth. Let it be drawn to you."

Rosalyn nodded.

We began by tuning the wands to the stone.

Rosalyn and I stood on either side of the Thread Stone.

I looked at Rosalyn. "On three?"

She nodded.

"One. Two…"

On three, we touched our wands to the Thread Stone. The effect was immediate and startling. A surge of magic rushed through me, so powerful it nearly took my breath away. My runes sparked to life beneath my shirt, glowing bright enough that their blue light was visible even through the fabric.

Across from me, Rosalyn gasped, her wings fluttering fast to help her keep her balance, shedding a cascade of glittering dust that seemed to be drawn toward the stone.

Her entire body took on a soft pink glow, just as when we'd made love.

The memory of that night sent another pulse of magic through me, and the Thread Stone responded, its glow intensifying.

"Focus," Kellen reminded us. "Visualize the Ley lines straightening. Bjorn, pull the frayed energy toward you. Rosalyn, be ready to thread the magic!"

I closed my eyes, picturing the twisted magical currents we'd seen on the map. In my mind, I reached for them, using my natural talent for fixing things to identify precisely where they had kinked and distorted. I could feel Rosalyn's magic on the other side of the stone, warm and vibrant like summer sunshine, while mine was calm and steady like a mountain stream. I worked hard, my heart pounding and my body sweating as I strained to pull the lines together. My footing fumbled as the stray stands sought to tear away from me and the wand.

"Steady," Kellen called. "Steady."

I heard the dryad speaking his people's tongue, and suddenly, my connection to the earth felt firmer, more rooted.

"I almost have it," I said, pulling the strands back into one massive, glowing blue-and-gold line of power, which sparked and bucked, wanting to rip away from me. But the wand kept it in line.

I took slow, deliberate steps as I tried to redirect the nearly combined lines toward the thread stone. The magic was chaos, wanting to pull away. I found myself straining, tugging at the power. I recited the runic enchantments over and over again.

On the other side of the stone, Rosalyn began to speak her own spells. I didn't know what charms they were, but they were light and airy, appearing like glimmering pink butterflies, the scent of cookies, scones, and baked bread drifting faintly toward me.

With my muscles straining, I pulled the magic into line and directed it through the Thread Stone.

"Rosalyn!" I called out to her in a warning.

The Ley lines slipped through the stone. When they did so, they intertwined once more. The air around us shimmered with magical energy.

"It's working!" Rosalyn exclaimed, holding her wand before her, pulling the magic through. But even as she spoke, the magic began to surge unpredictably. The beam of light splintered into a dozen smaller beams that shot off in different directions. Nearby plants suddenly sprouted flowers that bloomed and wilted in seconds. The ground beneath our feet trembled.

"Hold steady, Rosalyn!" Kellen called, extending his arms. "Bjorn, steady the magic. Keep it in line. Hold onto it for Rosalyn." Kellen recited enchantments loudly, green energy flowing from his hands, grounding the wild energy that bucked and kicked, yearning to break free. "Both of you hold on. The Ley lines are resisting!"

Kellen was right. I could feel a stubborn resistance as if the magic had grown accustomed to its disrupted state and was fighting our attempts to change it. Sweat beaded on my brow as I channeled more power into the Thread Stone.

"Rosalyn," I called to her, "we need more! You must pull harder."

She nodded, her face a mask of concentration. Her wings beat rapidly, generating more glittering dust that seemed to amplify the magic. The pink glow around her brightened, and I felt a surge in her magical output.

But the Ley lines resisted.

I could see the strain on Rosalyn's face.

I needed more magic. I had to hold the line to make it safer for Rosalyn.

Making up my mind, I drew upon the deep wells of magic I *never* accessed—the power that came with my royal blood. All royal family members carried special magic, but I never used mine. It was not *me*. I was not *that*. But now…to protect her, I dipped into that magic.

It responded at once.

My runes blazed brighter than ever, no longer just visible through my shirt but burning through the fabric itself, revealing the intricate patterns that marked me as a prince of the royal house of Frostfjord.

Rosalyn fluttered faster now and began to sing, her voice soft and welcoming. I didn't understand her words —they were pixie—but I guessed it to be one of her people's ancient songs. The aura around her softened, the forest floor blazing with flowers of every color. The air shimmered gold. Magical butterflies fluttered around her. It was a scene of beauty. Rosalyn's hair blazed bright red, the strands pulsing like living rubies. It was…mesmerizing.

The resistance suddenly gave way, like a knot finally coming untied.

The beam of light from the Thread Stone stabilized, taking on a prismatic quality. Through the hole in the center of the stone, I could see the Ley line finally weaving itself back together without resistance.

"The Ley line!" Kellen exclaimed. "It's realigning!"

A huge smile crossed Rosalyn's face.

Around us, chaos continued to reign as the magical discharge created all manner of strange effects. Trees temporarily turned crystalline and chimed like bells in the breeze. Flowers sprouted from Smoke's fur, making him sneeze sparks. Merry's horn shot tiny rainbows in all directions.

Working together, we gently pulled the Ley line back into its proper paths.

Just as the ritual neared its end, a voice called from the edge of the clearing. "What a magnificent sight!"

I saw Elder Thornberry from the corner of my eye, but I paid him no mind. My eyes were on Rosalyn, ensuring I held the last Ley line in check as it flowed toward her. Nothing mattered more than making sure she was safe.

While Rosalyn's magic was beautiful, it was also strong. With great skill, she coaxed the last of the magic through, tenderly helping it realign.

The magic between us straightened and began to flow like a calm river. A sound like a bell tolled, and the energy slowly sank back into the earth. I could see its glow traveling toward the standing stone where we had met the fairies.

The magic had been realigned.

"You can let go," Kellen called to us. "The work is done."

Breathing deeply, Rosalyn released the power.

Once I was sure she was safe, I also moved my wand away.

The runes on my body, however, still shimmered bright blue.

When Elder Thornberry looked at me, he gasped.

"Bjorn," he said. "Those runes! Those are the royal runes of Frostfjord! Why, my own father made me learn them as a child. Those are the runes of the royal house."

The words hung in the air. Across from me, I saw Rosalyn's eyes widen, her gaze fixed on runes now clearly visible on my arms and chest.

Elder Thornberry's expression went from one of confusion to a wide grin. "By golly, I knew you were too polite to simply be a Master of Horse. King Ramr and Queen Maren have a son named Bjorn. It's you, isn't it, Your Highness? You are Prince Bjorn?"

My gaze went to Rosalyn.

The instant she looked at me, she read the guilt on my face.

"Prince?" she whispered, the confusion in her voice cutting deeper than any blade.

"I..."

"Come, come," the elder said with a smile. "My word, it was very kind of your father to send one of his children to look after us! A royal prince in Moonshine Hollow? Well, isn't that something? And your royal magic seems to have helped us from a royal mess! Thank you, Prince Bjorn."

"*Prince* Bjorn," Rosalyn whispered.

I felt like my heart had dropped from my chest. And there it was… *Prince* Bjorn.

Before I could speak, the troupe of wild fairies appeared, their tiny forms darting through the clearing in patterns of evident joy. At the front of them glided a fairy man with a small, pointed cap with a red feather.

"Most wondrously done, O Charmed One, and thee, our cherished pixie friend," the fairy proclaimed, bowing low. "The veins of magic now flow true once more. From Her Radiance, our queen, I bring thee deepest gratitude."

"Charmed One?" Kellen repeated, looking at me with new understanding. "Of course. They recognize your royal magic."

"I…am honored to help," I told the fairy. "We all worked together."

Elder Thornberry stepped forward, his earlier shock replaced with something like awe.

"Gracious fairy friends, I send the greatest of respect and honor to your queen, and I thank you on behalf of all the citizens of Moonshine Hollow for your help."

"Of course, Elder Thornberry." The fairy then turned to Kellen. "Guardian," he said, giving the dryad a bow.

"Good Neighbor," the dryad replied, bowing in kind.

And with that, the fairies departed.

Elder Thornberry smiled widely at me. "Prince Bjorn of

Frostfjord in our humble hollow! What an honor. Prince, had I known your true identity—"

"Please," I said, finding my voice at last. "That's not… I didn't come here as a prince. I just came to help the unicorns."

But it was too late. The damage was done.

"I think I need to rest," Rosalyn said suddenly, her voice unnaturally even. "That took more out of me than I expected," she said with a forced laugh, then turned to Kellen. "Thank you for your guidance. And to you, Elder Thornberry, for your wisdom." She nodded politely to each of them. Finally, she looked at me. Her eyes shone with unshed tears, but her chin was held high. "Goodbye, Your Highness," she said, the formality a wall between us.

Before I could respond, she gathered Merry in his basket and took to the air, her wings carrying her swiftly away from the clearing.

"Oh my," Elder Thornberry said, looking between me and Rosalyn's retreating form. "Did I say something?"

Kellen placed a hand on the elder's shoulder. "Perhaps we should give Bjorn a moment," he suggested tactfully.

Alone in the clearing save for Smoke, I sank to my knees beside the Thread Stone. The runes on my skin still glowed faintly, though the intensity had faded with the ritual's completion.

One fairy that had dawdled at the back of the group, studying a flower the Ley line magic had caused to bloom, paused and looked back at me. Her brow furrowing, she joined me, hovering in front of me.

"Thou hast done most admirably, Charmed Prince,"

she said, studying me with eyes ancient as starlight. "And yet, methinks thy heart is now as tangled as the Ley lines once were."

"Can you fix it?" I asked, only half in jest.

She shook her tiny head. "Some magicks lie beyond even our ken. The heart's path must be walked by its bearer alone. Yet, as with the Ley lines, 'tis courage that begins the mending," she said, laying a delicate hand on my shoulder. "Our deepest gratitude is thine. The balance is restored. Now go and restore thine own world."

She gave me a crooked smile and then disappeared, leaving me with my thoughts and regrets.

Smoke nudged my hand with his nose, whining softly.

"I know, boy," I said, scratching behind his ears. "I've made a mess of things." I looked in the direction Rosalyn had flown. "But maybe it's better this way. A clean break."

Yet even as I said the words, I knew they weren't true. Nothing about it felt right.

The Ley lines might've been fixed, but the connection that mattered most to me was more broken than ever.

And I had no one to blame but myself.

CHAPTER 17
ROSALYN

I slammed another ball of dough onto my flour-dusted counter with perhaps more force than necessary. The kitchen was hot, even with the door open to the cool evening air. I'd flown straight back from the Whispering Woods and immediately started baking, my favorite way of coping with emotional turmoil. The Sconery was filled with the scent of my Forget Me scones, a recipe I'd created for customers suffering from heartache.

"Stupid royal runes," I muttered, pounding the dough with my fist. "Stupid prince. Stupid me for not realizing the absurdly handsome man with perfect manners might possibly be more than a unicorn expert."

Merry watched from his perch on top of the flour canister, his tail swishing back and forth, sending up little clouds of white with each movement.

"Don't judge me," I told him. "You didn't figure it out either."

He meowed in what sounded suspiciously like disagreement.

"Oh, so now you're claiming you knew all along? Funny, I don't recall you warning me before I made a fool of myself."

The recipe had taken me months to perfect. A pinch of ground starshade petals collected during a waning moon for dulling painful memories, crushed strawberry blossom crystal for sweetening bitter thoughts, and just a hint of silverleaf dust for bringing clarity. They wouldn't make anyone truly forget, of course. That kind of magic was both dangerous and dishonest. But they eased the sharp edges of heartbreak, making the pain more bearable until time could do its work.

"Maybe I need to eat the entire batch myself," I said, violently shaping the dough. "One for every minute I spent thinking about his lips, one for every time I imagined our future together, and at least three for that night in the cabin that I am definitely not thinking about right now."

I sighed.

"*Prince* Bjorn," I repeated for the hundredth time, testing how the words felt in my mouth. "I slept with a prince." I groaned, dropping my head onto the counter with a soft thud, not caring about the flour in my hair. "And now I'm talking to myself. Great. Clearly going insane is the next logical step."

Prince Bjorn. Not Bjorn Runeson, Master of Horse, but Prince Bjorn of Frostfjord. The blue runes blazing on his skin, the same ones that had glowed when we made love, weren't just any Rune elf markings—they were royal markings. Everything made sense now: his formal manners, careful speech, and reluctance to talk about his family.

The mother.

She was a freaking queen, not just an overbearing mom.

"Ugh! Burnt ends!"

"Dear me," Winifred called, her voice cutting through my internal tirade. She took one look at me—flour-dusted, red-eyed, surrounded by enough scones to feed half of Moonshine Hollow—and sighed. Winifred hung her enormous hat on a peg by the door and rolled up her sleeves. "Put the kettle on. You look like you could use some tea."

I didn't argue, just set a pot of water to boil with a flick of my fingers. Winifred busied herself clearing a space at the counter, moving aside bowls and baking sheets with brisk efficiency.

"I'm guessing you've been at this since you returned from the Whispering Woods?" she asked.

I nodded, wiping my hands on my apron. "How did you know I was there?"

"Small town, big ears," she said with a shrug. "Word travels fast, especially when it involves fairies, magical disturbances, and secret royalty."

I winced at the last part. "So, everyone knows?"

"That you and our mysterious visitor from the north fixed the Ley lines? Yes. That the man who's been making eyes at you since he arrived is actually Prince Bjorn of

Frostfjord? Also yes. Did you really think Elder Thornberry would keep that to himself?" She paused, fixing me with a pointed look. "That the two of you spent a night together at Woodsong Cabin? Not yet, but give it time."

My face flushed so hot I was surprised the flour on my cheeks didn't bake right off. "That's—we didn't—well, we did, but—oh, burnt ends!"

The kettle whistled, and I gratefully turned away to make the tea.

"Forget Me scones?" Winifred asked, eyeing them with an arched brow. "Rather drastic, don't you think?"

"I needed to bake something," I said then fixed us both a cup of tea, setting Winnie's before her.

"Mmm." She took a sip of her tea. "You know, I've been suspicious of our northern friend since I first saw him lurking outside your shop."

"Yes, I know. I should have listened."

"I saw him at the market with a big man who called him *Prince* Bjorn…"

I nearly choked on my tea. "You knew?"

"That he was royal? Not at first. But that he was hiding something? Absolutely." Winifred helped herself to a scone, breaking it in half and watching the blue magic curl like smoke from its center. "So, I kept an eye on him. That's how I learned the truth. I confronted him about it, right out there in the street."

My heart thumped painfully in my chest. "What did he say?"

"Not much, directly."

"Why didn't you tell me?" I asked, unable to keep the hurt from my voice.

"Because I was still gathering intelligence," Winifred said matter-of-factly. "Also, I needed to determine whether he was a threat or just an idiot."

"And your conclusion?"

"Idiot," she said promptly. "But not a malicious one. Just a man who's made a mess of things because he's scared."

"Royal *Prince* Bjorn, scared of a pixie baker?"

"Terrified," Winifred said. "Absolutely petrified. You should have seen his face when I confronted him. He looked like he'd rather face a fire-breathing dragon than risk you finding out who he really was."

"But why? It makes no sense. He lied. To everyone. To me. He let me think he was just…just a normal person. Just Bjorn."

"And you wish he'd told you he was a prince?"

"Yes!" I exclaimed, then hesitated. "Wait. Wait… Okay, no. I don't know." I paced the small kitchen, narrowly avoiding knocking over a jar of dried lavender. "I mean, if he'd introduced himself as Prince Bjorn of Frostfjord, wielder of royal magic, owner of fifty fancy fur-trimmed cloaks, I'd have—" I stopped short, realizing what I was saying.

"You'd have what?" Winifred prompted, looking amused.

"I'd have acted differently with him," I admitted. I groaned, covering my face with my hands, forgetting they were covered in flour. "Oh, gods. I had a one-night stand with a prince. My mother would faint dead away."

"Knowing he was a prince, would you have flirted with him, invited him to dinner, been yourself with him?"

I opened my mouth to say "of course I would have," then closed it again. Would I? Or would I have been intimidated, formal, careful? Would I have asked all the same questions, shared all the same stories, kissed him in the rain-soaked cabin with the same abandon?

"I think he wanted you to know *him*," Winifred continued. "Not his title. Just him."

"But who is he? The real Bjorn?" I sank onto a stool. "Was any of it real?"

"My dear," Winifred said dryly, "I may be the town gossip, but even I don't have the supernatural ability to determine a man's sincerity. Though if I did, I'd be much richer and probably married to that handsome merchant who passed through last summer. That said, I think it's possible that the Bjorn you know is far more real than whatever princely version exists in Frostfjord. From what I can tell, he came here to escape all that."

I thought about our time together. The way he'd smiled when I made him dinner, how he'd asked genuine questions about my baking, the tender way he'd touched me in the darkness of the cabin. The vulnerability in his eyes when he'd told me there were things about him I didn't know.

"When we first met at Elder Thornberry's," I said quietly, "he seemed so uncomfortable with all the attention." I paused, remembering the moment.

"That is telling."

"But then his glowing runes. I mean... That was over the top in terms of a lie."

"His runes glowed when he was with you?"

I nodded.

"Dear, that's not something he can control. That's a sign of love."

"I thought he was just excited to see me. You know, in a state of...undress." I felt my cheeks heat again. "But his arms practically lit up the whole cabin when we, um... Well, you know."

"Did they now? My, my."

"Not helping, Winifred!"

"On the contrary, I'm providing valuable context for your romantic crisis," she said. "That's more than just attraction, dear."

"I didn't fall in love with a prince," I murmured, more to myself than to Winifred. "I fell in love with a man who helped unicorns, who was kind to Merry, who fixed my teacup when it broke."

Winifred's eyes widened. "Love, is it? We've progressed from 'that handsome Rune elf' to love rather quickly."

I hadn't meant to say that word aloud, but I couldn't take it back now that it was out. And I didn't want to. Because it was true. Somewhere between that first meeting at Elder Thornberry's and our night in the cabin. I had fallen completely in love with Bjorn.

Not Prince Bjorn. Just Bjorn.

I sighed heavily. "You've seen him, Winnie. Those shoulders alone could inspire sonnets."

"I'm old, dear, not blind," Winifred said. "Though I suspect your feelings run deeper than an appreciation for his physique."

I sighed, tracing the rim of my teacup with one finger. "He still should have told me."

"Yes, he should have," Winifred agreed. "But secrets have a way of becoming harder to tell the longer they're kept."

I thought about the fear in his eyes this morning, the way he'd said there were things about him I didn't know, his promise that he would tell me soon. He'd been working up to it.

"What would you have done?" Winifred asked. "If you were a royal, tired of being seen only for your title, and you'd found someone who saw you for yourself?"

I tried to imagine it—the weight of a crown, the expectations, the loneliness of being surrounded by people who saw only your position. How tempting would it be to pretend for a little while that you were free?

"I'd probably do exactly what he did," I admitted reluctantly. "Though I'd like to think I'd have come clean before...well, you know. Before things got complicated."

"Complicated meaning horizontal?" Winifred suggested innocently.

"Winifred!"

"What? I was young once, too, you know. But with your wings, would it be vertical?"

"Please stop."

Winifred chuckled. "So, what will you do?"

"I don't know." I turned my teacup in my hands, watching the leaves swirl at the bottom. "He's still a prince. His life is in Frostfjord. Mine is here."

"Sometimes," Winifred said softly, "love requires us to reimagine what we thought our lives would be."

I looked around my kitchen: flour-dusted counters, shelves of spices and magical ingredients, stacks of recipe books. The Sconery was everything I'd worked for, my dream realized. Could I leave it behind for love? Would Bjorn even ask me to?

"He probably thinks I hate him now," I said with a sigh.

"Then you should tell him otherwise," Winifred suggested. "Don't be prideful like Miss Beth," she said with a grin, referring to the heroine of *Crown and Crumpets*.

She was right, as usual. If there was any chance for Bjorn and me, one of us would have to be brave enough to reach out first. And since he'd probably convinced himself he'd ruined everything...

"I'll go see him tomorrow," I decided. "I deserve an explanation, and he deserves a chance to give one."

Winifred smiled, satisfied. "Good. Now, what are you going to do with all these scones?"

For the first time in hours, I laughed. "I may have gotten a bit carried away."

"A bit?" Winifred raised an eyebrow, looking around at the dozens of glowing pastries.

"Fine, I got a lot carried away." I stood, feeling lighter than I had since Elder Thornberry exposed Bjorn's secret.

"Would you like to take some home? I'll sell the rest tomorrow at a discount."

As we wrapped up a few scones for Winifred, I felt a strange sense of peace settling over me. The hurt hadn't disappeared but had transformed into something more nuanced.

"Winifred," I said suddenly, "thank you."

She waved a dismissive hand. "For what? Sticking my nose where it doesn't belong? I do that for everyone in town."

"For caring enough to stick your nose in," I corrected her with a smile. "And for helping me see past my hurt to what really matters."

"Well, someone has to keep you young people from making a mess of things. Life is too short for foolish pride and unnecessary misunderstandings." She paused at the door. "And if you do marry him, I expect an invitation to the royal wedding. Front row, not stuck behind some giant ambassador from the Northern Reach."

"I promise, Winnie."

Winifred winked and then departed.

I locked up the shop and made my way upstairs to my apartment. Merry was curled up on my bed, his little horn still occasionally shooting tiny sparks—an aftereffect of the wild magic from earlier.

"What do you think, Mer-Mer?" I asked, scratching under his chin. "Should I give our prince another chance?"

Merry purred, his blue eyes blinking slowly at me.

"Very helpful."

I caught sight of myself in the mirror and grimaced.

Flour dusted my hair, cheeks, and apron. I looked like I'd lost a fight with a bakery.

"If I'm going to confront royalty tomorrow, I should probably look less like a disaster area," I murmured, heading for the bath.

Running the water into my claw-footed bathtub, I sprinkled in some relaxing bath salts mixed with dried flower petals, one of Juniper's creations. Pulling off my clothes, I stepped into the bath, letting the warm water envelope me. Deep sensations of relaxation washed over me as I inhaled the floral scents of the flowers mixed with the steam. Snapping my wet fingers, I set the candles sitting around the room to light.

As I washed away the evidence of my stress-baking, I rehearsed what I would say to Bjorn tomorrow. There were still so many questions. He said he didn't have a girlfriend. Was he being honest? Why had he really come to Moonshine Hollow? What did his royal duties entail? Could there be any future for us across such different worlds?

"Your Royal Highness," I addressed the absent man. "I kindly request an explanation for your deception."

I sighed.

This was ridiculous.

I was ridiculous.

The whole situation was ridiculous.

But beneath all the jokes and questions, there was a simpler truth: I missed him. I missed his quiet strength, his gentle humor, the way his eyes crinkled when he smiled. I missed the man who had held me through the night as if I were something precious. I could imagine him in my bathtub, sitting across from me, the pair of us grinning stupidly at one another.

Prince or not, I loved the man behind the title. And tomorrow, I would find out the truth.

I could only hope that he wanted me as much as I wanted him.

CHAPTER 18

BJORN

The ceiling in my guest room at Elder Thornberry's estate had a fascinating water stain. If I squinted just right, it resembled a unicorn or possibly a lopsided rabbit. I'd been staring at it for hours, having not slept all night. The events in the Whispering Woods kept replaying in my mind: the Ley lines shifting back into place, Elder Thornberry's excited exclamation, and the expression on Rosalyn's face. The hurt in her eyes had been unmistakable. Her formal "Your Highness" was like a dagger to my heart.

Smoke whined sympathetically from his spot at the foot of my bed.

"Yeah, I know. I really messed up," I said with a sad sigh.

Reaching out with his paw, Smoke batted my leg.

I reached down and gave him a pat, grateful for the

support, even though my stomach was twisting with dread.

My bag was already packed. After returning to the estate yesterday, I'd done my best to avoid the elder's enthusiastic questions about my royal heritage, pleading exhaustion from the magical work. He'd been understanding, though clearly bursting with curiosity. I couldn't face another day of it, not when each polite "Prince Bjorn" from the elder's staff reminded me of how Rosalyn had reacted.

The magical task I'd come to accomplish was complete. The Ley lines were realigned, the unicorns would recover, and Moonshine Hollow would return to normal. There was no reason for me to stay, especially now that my secret was out and Rosalyn wanted nothing to do with me.

I'd spent half the night writing and discarding letters to her. Apologies, explanations, declarations. None of them seemed adequate. How could I explain that I'd lied to her because I wanted her to see me, not my title? That, for the first time in my life, I'd felt like myself with her? That I'd fallen hopelessly in love with her?

Ultimately, I'd burned all the letters in the small fireplace and decided to leave early the next morning. A clean break would be best for both of us.

Dawn had barely broken when I went downstairs, hoping to speak with Elder Thornberry before departing. Despite the early hour, the elder was already up, enjoying a bountiful breakfast on his veranda.

"Prince Bjorn!" he exclaimed, jumping to his feet with surprising agility. "What a pleasant surprise! I was just telling my wife about your remarkable magical display yesterday. Please, join us for breakfast."

"I'm afraid I can't stay," I said, bowing politely. "I came to bid you farewell and express my gratitude for your hospitality. With the Ley lines restored, I must return to Frostfjord."

The elder's face fell. "So soon? But we'd hoped to host a celebration in your honor! The citizens of Moonshine Hollow would love to properly thank their royal savior."

The thought of being paraded around town as "the royal savior" made my stomach turn.

"You're very kind, but I must decline. My father will be expecting me." This wasn't entirely true—I'd left Frostfjord without specifying when I'd return—but Elder Thornberry didn't need to know that.

"Well, if duty calls," the elder said, looking disappointed. "But you must promise to visit us again. Right, dear?" he asked his wife.

Petunia nodded enthusiastically. "Moonshine Hollow will always welcome you, Prince Bjorn."

"Thank you. The town has been…unforgettable."

From the corner of my eye, I caught a flicker of movement. Emmalyn stood at the edge of the veranda, her expression unreadable. When our eyes met, she gave me a long, measured look before hurrying away.

Something about her hasty departure made me uneasy, but I had no time to dwell on it. After exchanging some pleasantries with Elder Thornberry and his wife, I set off for the docks, Smoke trotting dutifully beside me.

The morning air was fresh and cool, laden with the

scent of blooming flowers and baking bread. I tried not to think about how much the latter reminded me of Rosalyn, of her warm smile and flour-dusted hands.

As I reached the harbor, I spotted the riverboat preparing to depart. According to the harbormaster I'd spoken with late last night, it would be bound for Port Silverleaf, where I could catch a larger ship to Frostfjord.

"Almost out of here, boy," I told Smoke, who seemed less than enthusiastic about our departure.

The truth was, I'd miss everything about Moonshine Hollow—the magical charm of the place, the friendly townsfolk who'd treated me like a regular person, the unicorns and fairies, and most of all, a certain pixie baker whose laughter had become my favorite sound in the world.

But wishes and regrets changed nothing. I'd lied to her, betrayed her trust, and now I had to live with the consequences.

I had just reached the gangplank when I heard someone shouting my name.

"Prince Bjorn! Wait!"

Turning, I was surprised to see Winifred hurrying toward me, her enormous hat bobbing precariously as she ran. Behind her came Emmalyn, clutching her side like she'd been sprinting.

"Don't you dare get on that boat, young man!" Winifred called, wagging a finger at me as she approached. Despite being a third of my height, she managed to look impressively intimidating.

"I beg your pardon?" I said, genuinely confused.

Emmalyn reached us, panting. "Rosalyn," she gasped out. "She was going to see you this morning. She was planning to try to work things out."

My heart skipped a beat. "She was?"

"Yes," Winifred said with annoyance. "And I will not let you sail away like some coward before she can speak her mind."

"I'm not a coward," I protested, stung by the accusation even though a small voice in my head whispered that she wasn't entirely wrong. "I'm trying to do what's best for everyone."

"Best for everyone?" Winifred scoffed. "Or easiest for you?"

I winced. The gnome's words hit uncomfortably close to the mark.

"Look," Emmalyn said, her breathing finally returning to normal, "Aside from the lying, I don't know exactly what happened between you and Rosalyn, but I know my friend genuinely cares for you. She deserves a chance to say what she needs to say. You owe her that much."

"I spoke to her this morning," Winifred said. "She was getting ready to visit you at the elder's estate. If you hurry, you can catch her before she leaves. Don't leave things like this. Rosalyn deserves better."

She was right, of course. Running away without giving Rosalyn a chance to speak her piece was cowardly. But what if she just wanted to tell me how much I'd hurt and disappointed her? I wasn't sure I could bear it.

"Fix this," Winifred said, meeting my gaze. Her look was piercing. "For her…and for you, *Bjorn*."

"Yes... Yes, you're right."

"Oh! Oh, I know," Emmalyn said, then reached into the bag Winifred was carrying and extracted...a book?

Winifred and Emmalyn exchanged glances, both of them smiling excitedly.

"Perfect! Perfect idea," Winifred told Emmalyn then turned to me. "Here," Winifred said, taking the book from Emmalyn and thrusting it into my hands. "Read chapter fifty-eight."

"Chapter...chapter fifty-eight?" I looked down at the worn volume, its cover depicting a crown resting atop what appeared to be a pastry. The title read *Crown and Crumpets*.

"Right. Chapter fifty-eight," Emmalyn agreed. "This is Rosalyn's favorite book. Read it. You'll understand."

Feeling distinctly confused but seeing no other option, I opened the book to the indicated chapter and began to scan the text. It seemed to be some sort of romantic scene where the male protagonist, a royal lord, finally revealed his true identity—and his real feelings—to the baker's daughter with whom he'd fallen in love. After much emotional back-and-forth, he proposed marriage in a grand gesture.

It was, frankly, a bit over-the-top for my northern sensibilities. Still, as I continued reading, something else caught my attention... The similarities between Lord Thornwick's and Miss Beth's situation and mine were uncanny. He, too, had hidden his identity, fearing he would never be loved for himself rather than his title, but Miss Beth *had* fallen in love with him.

"Do you understand now?" Winifred asked impatiently.

I looked up from the book, my mind racing. "I do," I said tepidly, and then a broad smile crossed my face. "I do! By the Nine Gods, I'm an idiot. Where am I going?" I said, gesturing to the boat. "But I can't just march up to her bakery and propose like Lord Thornwick, can I? Rosalyn's probably furious with me."

"She is," Winifred confirmed cheerfully. "She spent the whole night baking Forget Me scones. *But* she's also in love with you."

"She... What?"

"Love, you thick-headed northern fool. She's in love. With you."

"Winifred has a unique way of expressing herself," Emmalyn interjected diplomatically, "but she's right about Rosalyn's feelings. And if you feel the same way, you need to show her. Rosalyn is a romantic. This *will* work."

Of course I loved Rosalyn. I loved her warmth, her kindness, and her talent for making everyone around her feel special. I loved that she saw me as Bjorn, not as Prince Bjorn. I loved how she'd opened her world to me without hesitation, even when she'd thought I was just a visiting horse master.

"I do love her," I said simply. "I do."

"Well, then," Winifred said, planting her hands on her hips, "what are you waiting for? Special royal permission?"

Smoke barked his agreement, his tail wagging excitedly.

"But I need to—" I gestured vaguely at myself, suddenly conscious of my travel-worn appearance. "Wait, I have my ceremonial clothes in my bag."

Emmalyn's eyes lit up. "I know what to do. Come with me. Winnie, don't let Rosalyn leave. I'll be back with Bjorn in a heartbeat."

"Where are we going?"

"Thistle and Thyme, so you can get ready."

"Leave Rosalyn to me," Winifred said.

"Come on, Your Highness. We've got a royal proposal to arrange," Emmalynn said, taking me by the arm and pulling me away.

An hour later, I stood outside The Sconery and Teashop, dressed in my formal Rune elf attire: a gray-blue tunic embroidered with silver runes, formal dress trousers, a cloak with fur trim, and the silver torc that marked my royal status. My hair was neatly combed and braided, and my beard was trimmed, courtesy of Tansy's quick work with scissors. I even smelled good, thanks to whatever Juniper had sprayed me with. In my hands, I clutched an enormous bouquet of moonblush roses and silverstar lilies that Winifred had given me.

I felt ridiculous.

I also felt like I might throw up.

"Stop fidgeting," Winifred hissed from her hiding spot

behind a nearby cart. "You look like you're about to face execution, not propose to the woman you love."

"The two feel remarkably similar at the moment," I muttered.

"Remember," Emmalyn whispered from her position near The Sconery's side door, "sing the song to get her attention, then speak from the heart."

"Right. Sing." I cleared my throat, trying to summon the Song of Runeheart, the traditional anthem of our royal house. The problem was that I'd always been hopeless at music. Asa used to joke that my singing voice could curdle milk. But my mother had insisted I learned. So, even though I sounded like a croaking frog, I knew the tune.

It would be a disaster, but for Rosalyn, I would try.

Taking a deep breath, I began to sing, my voice cracking embarrassingly:

"From ice and stone, our halls were hewn,
"Where northern stars o'er mountains gleam.
"The Runeheart line, steadfast and true,
"Doth guard the realm and shape the dream."

Several passersby had stopped to stare, their expressions ranging from curiosity to alarm. Then, I saw a flash of movement in an upstairs window of The Sconery. A moment later, Rosalyn appeared, her red hair catching the morning sunlight.

She looked down at me, her eyes widening in surprise.

Opening her window, she looked out. "Bjorn?" she called, her voice carrying a note of confusion. "What are you doing?"

"The wind may howl, the sea may rise,

"But still we stand through storm and tide.
"By flame and frost, by oath and steel,
"Our hearts hold fast, our strength our guide."

A wide smile crossed Rosalyn's face as she took in the scene.

"Though far we roam on wind and wave,
"The northern lights shall guide us home.
"In every fjord, our name resounds.
"The Runeheart blood, the sea's true throne."

"Bjorn…"

Now or never.

I abandoned my mangled attempt at the royal anthem and stepped forward, clutching the flowers so tightly I was probably crushing their stems.

"Rosalyn," I called up to her. "I came to tell you the truth. All of it."

Her expression softened slightly, and she sat on the windowsill, her wings catching the light. "I'm listening."

"My name is Bjorn Runeheart, third son of King Ramr and Queen Maren of Frostfjord." The formality of the introduction felt strange after weeks of being just Bjorn, but I forced myself to continue. "I came to Moonshine Hollow because I was tired of being seen only as a prince, never as myself. I wanted to know if I could be something more than my title."

I paused, gathering my courage. "And then I met you. You saw me…just *me*. Not a prince, not a royal treasury, not a pawn, just Bjorn. And for the first time in my life, I felt like I was exactly where I belonged."

Rosalyn's expression was unreadable from this

distance, but she hadn't slammed the window shut, which I chose to take as an encouraging sign.

"I should have told you who I was. I wanted to, especially after…after the cabin," I said, making the crowd around me whisper, but I continued. "But I was afraid of losing what we had. In trying to protect myself, I hurt you. For that, I am truly, deeply sorry.

"If you can find it in your heart to forgive me," I continued, my voice growing stronger, "I promise I will never lie to you again. I promise to be worthy of your trust. Because the truth is, Rosalyn Hartwood, I love you. I love your kindness, your laughter, your talent for making everyone around you feel special. I love that you can make magic with flour and butter. I love that you have a glitter-sneezing caticorn as your best friend. I love you. I love you, Rosalyn."

A smile tugged at her lips, and her eyes looked glossy with unshed tears.

"I understand if you can't forgive me. I understand if this is goodbye. But maybe…maybe not. Maybe this is a beginning instead. Maybe…" I took a deep breath, then went for it. "Rosalyn Hartwood, will you be my princess?"

There was a moment of absolute silence. Even the crowd that had gathered seemed to hold its breath.

Rosalyn gave me a soft smile. "No, Bjorn," she called.

My heart plummeted until she continued.

"I don't need to be your *princess*, but I would be thrilled to be your wife, your partner, married to Bjorn of Frostfjord. I love you. I don't care if you are a prince or not."

The crowd let out a collective cheer.

Smoke barked excitedly.

"Really?" I called, hardly daring to believe it. "You forgive me?"

"Yes. I love you, you royal idiot."

At that moment, Winifred stepped forward, her hands weaving an intricate pattern in the air. Green vines suddenly shot up the side of The Sconery, twisting and growing at an unnatural speed until they formed a sturdy, living ladder that led to Rosalyn's window.

"Climb," Emmalyn urged me, making shooing motions with her hands. "Just like in the book."

Winifred casted once more, the spell causing the entire front of Rosalyn's shop to be covered in bright pink soullock roses.

Rosalyn gasped.

"Go on, Lord Thornwick," Emmalyn told me.

I hesitated only a moment before tucking the flowers under one arm and climbing up. The vines were surprisingly sturdy, holding my weight easily as I made my way up to Rosalyn's window. When I reached her, she was smiling through tears, her wings fluttering with emotion.

"Oh, Bjorn," she whispered softly.

"I'm truly sorry," I told her.

"I know," she replied. "Otherwise, you'd never let Emmalyn and Winifred talk you into the Thornwick and Beth proposal scene," she said then wrapped her arms around me, placing a sweet and soft kiss on my lips. I nearly dropped the flowers in my eagerness to hold her, one arm wrapping around her waist while the other still clutched the bouquet.

Below us, the crowd cheered. I vaguely registered Winifred doing something with her hands, and suddenly, a burst of rose petals exploded all around us, tiny pink sparks shooting off into the sky.

Everyone below called out excitedly, whooping and clapping.

When we finally broke apart, Rosalyn grinned at me. "You do realize everyone in town will talk about this for years, right? A Prince of Frostfjord, climbing up to the pixie baker's window on a magical vine ladder."

"Let them talk," I said, surprising myself with how little I cared about the spectacle we'd made. "All I want is for you to be happy. As long as you're happy, nothing else matters."

Her eyes softened. "I *am* happy. I love you, Bjorn."

"I love you too."

Whatever challenges lay ahead, my duties in Frostfjord, her business in Moonshine Hollow, the inevitable meeting with my family, we would face them together. We would make this work because sometimes true love was just as magical as the tales in storybooks.

CHAPTER 19
ROSALYN

I couldn't stop smiling.
Even as Bjorn moved away from the window, joining me inside, my cheeks hurt from grinning like a fool. Merry watched us with his usual judgmental stare. Still, even he seemed affected by the moment, his little horn softly glowing pink as he flicked his tail and pretended not to care about the romantic scene he'd just witnessed.

Bjorn stood in the middle of my apartment, looking regal but also adorably uncomfortable in his royal attire. The silver torc around his neck gleamed in the morning sunlight streaming through the window, and the blue of his tunic made his eyes even more striking.

But the expression on his face took my breath away—a mixture of joy, relief, and love so intense it made my heart skip. Those same blue eyes that had looked at me with desire in the cabin now held something deeper, more profound. And this time, there were no secrets between us.

"Well," I said, trying for lightness but hearing the breathless quality in my voice, "that was…"

"Awful? Embarrassing?"

"Perfect," I assured him, reaching up to touch his face. "*Crown and Crumpets*. Chapter fifty-eight."

"Did I live up to the literary standard?"

"You exceeded it," I assured him, rising onto my tiptoes to press my lips against his.

Bjorn's arms slipped around my waist, drawing me closer. "I was desperate. When Winifred told me you were coming to see me, that you didn't hate me…"

"I *was* angry," I admitted. "And hurt. But I could never hate you, Bjorn." My wings fluttered nervously as I gathered my courage. "I meant what I said. I love you. The prince part is… Well, it will take some getting used to, but it doesn't change how I feel."

"Rosalyn," he whispered, then pulled me close, kissing me deeply.

This kiss was different from the others. There was no spell from mischievous unicorns, rain-soaked desperation, or secrets. We were just Bjorn and Rosalyn, with nothing hidden or held back.

His lips were gentle at first, almost reverent, but they grew more insistent when I pressed myself closer.

I don't know how long we stood there, lost in each other, but eventually, we broke apart, both breathing hard. Bjorn rested his forehead against mine, his eyes closed as though savoring the moment.

"I should have told you the truth from the beginning," he whispered. "I was so afraid of losing you."

"I understand why you didn't," I said softly. "And I forgive you."

His eyes opened, searching mine. "Just like that?"

"Well, the dramatic proposal and terrible singing didn't hurt," I teased. "But I understand wanting to be seen for yourself, not what others expect you to be."

Understanding dawned in his eyes. "Spring Haven. You left because you wanted to be a baker, not a butterfly maiden."

I nodded. "We're not so different after all."

"I meant what I said outside. I want to marry you, Rosalyn. But I need you to understand what that would mean. My life in Frostfjord… It's complicated. There would be expectations, duties…"

"Are you trying to talk me out of accepting your proposal?" I asked, raising an eyebrow.

"No!" he said quickly. "I just want you to know what you'd be getting into. My mother can be…formidable. The court politics are exhausting. And the weather—"

"I know we have a lot to figure out, but we'll do it together."

Relief flooded his features. "Together," he agreed, pulling me close again.

This time when we kissed, the gentle exploration gave way to something more urgent. The relief of reconciliation combined into a heady mixture that left us both breathless. My fingers found the clasps of his formal cloak, pushing it off his shoulders and onto the floor. His hands, meanwhile, had found their way beneath my blouse and were skimming over the sensitive skin of my waist.

"Rosalyn," he breathed against my lips, "are you sure? About everything?"

The vulnerability in his voice made my heart ache. Even now, part of him expected rejection, feared I might change my mind once the romantic moment had passed.

In answer, I took his hand and led him toward my bedroom. Sensing what was about to happen, Merry sauntered away, his dignity intact.

Sunlight streamed through the gauzy curtains, bathing the small room in a soft glow. My bedroom was cozy, filled with mismatched furniture I'd collected over the years, the magenta-colored walls adorned with framed pressed flowers, embroidered scenes, and sketches from my friends. It wasn't grand or royal, but it was mine.

Bjorn looked around with interest, taking in the personal touches: the stack of cookbooks beside the bed, the vase of ever-blooming pinkie tulips that Juniper had given me last solstice, the tiny caticorn figurine that had been my first purchase when I'd moved to Moonshine Hollow.

"Sorry," I said with a soft grin. "It's not every day a girl invites a prince into her bedroom. If I had known you were coming, I would have dusted," I said with a laugh.

"It's perfect. It's…it's you."

I smiled softly at him then reached up and carefully removed the silver torc from around his neck, setting it on my dresser. Then I began to undo the intricate fastenings of his royal tunic, my fingers working deftly. "And you… You're still Bjorn—*just* Bjorn—to me," I whispered.

He pulled me against the warmth of his now-bare chest. The blue runes that marked his skin began to glow, responding to my touch. I traced one with my finger, following its path across his collarbone.

"These are beautiful," I murmured.

"They *only* glow when I'm with you."

The intensity of his gaze made my heart race. My wings fluttered involuntarily, shedding sparkling dust that seemed to be drawn to his glowing runes, creating an ethereal dance of light between us.

"Maybe it's magic," I suggested, only half-joking. "Northern and southern magic, finding balance."

His smile turned tender. "Maybe it's just love."

We kissed again, this time more urgently. Working quickly, we removed the rest of our clothing. Soon, Bjorn's hands were roving my now-bare skin. I felt that familiar rush of warmth spreading through me, my body responding to his touch.

Just as in the cabin, my skin took on a soft pink glow, shimmering more intensely as his hands explored my body. Bjorn's runes flared bright blue in response, the patterns spreading further across his skin. Where our bodies touched, the colors merged into a stunning purple that bathed the room in otherworldly light.

Bjorn lay me gently on the bed, his eyes darkening as they roamed over me. "I've dreamed of having you like this again," he whispered.

"Show me," I urged, pulling him closer.

He kissed me deeply, then began a torturously slow journey down my body, his lips and tongue leaving trails of fire on my skin. I moaned in pleasure when he reached my breasts. He took his time, lavishing attention on each one until I was arching off the bed, desperate for more. The pink glow of my skin intensified where his mouth touched as if my magic was reaching for his.

"Bjorn," I gasped, tangling my fingers in his hair. "Please."

He glanced up, a wicked smile on his face that was so unlike his usual reserved demeanor it sent another wave of heat coursing through me. "Patience, my love. I plan to worship every inch of you."

And he did, moving lower with deliberate slowness that had me writhing beneath him, my wings beating so fast they lifted my hips off the bed. When he finally settled between my thighs, the first touch of his tongue against the soft folds of my core nearly undid me completely.

I cried out, not caring who might hear. My hands gripped the sheets as the pleasure built inside me, coiling tighter with each delicious stroke of his tongue. The glow of my skin pulsed in rhythm with my heartbeat, growing brighter as I approached the edge.

Just when I thought I couldn't take anymore, Bjorn slid his fingers inside me as his tongue continued its relentless assault. The dual sensation pushed me over the edge, my release washing over me in waves as I called out his name. The pink glow of my skin flashed, sending cascades of magical sparks into the air.

Before I'd fully recovered, Bjorn was moving up my

body, his eyes blazing with need, his runes glowing so brightly they cast shadows on the walls.

"I need you," he groaned, kissing my neck. "Now."

"Yes," I breathed, wrapping my legs around his waist.

He entered me in one smooth thrust, both of us gasping at the perfect fit of our bodies. For a moment, he remained still, his face pressed against my neck, our breaths mingling. The place where we joined glowed purple, our magics intertwining just as our bodies did.

"I love you," he whispered, his voice filled with wonder.

"I love you too," I replied, my hands sliding down his back to urge him closer.

He moved then, setting a rhythm that immediately made me climb toward another peak. Bjorn's hands gripped my hips. His control was slipping, his thrusts becoming more urgent as his runes blazed brighter. I could feel the tension building in his body, matching my own rising pleasure.

"Rosalyn," he gasped, his voice strained.

I clutched his shoulders. "I want to feel you, Bjorn. Give me all of you… Bjorn…"

He captured my mouth in a searing kiss as his movements became erratic. When his release finally came, he groaned my name against my lips, the sound pushing me over the edge for a second time.

The intensity of our combined climax sent a surge of magical energy through the room, making the small objects on my dresser rattle and the curtains billow as if caught in a sudden breeze.

As the waves of pleasure gradually subsided, we lay together, our breathing ragged and our skin slick with sweat. Bjorn's weight on top of me was comforting rather than crushing, and I held him close, not wanting to break our connection just yet.

"That was…" he began, then seemed at a loss for words.

"Magical?" I suggested with a breathless laugh.

He lifted his head to smile down at me, his eyes filled with such tenderness it made my heart ache. "Definitely magical." He brushed a strand of hair from my face, his touch gentle. "And just the beginning."

Eventually, he rolled to the side but kept me tucked against him, his arm around me, my head on his chest where I could hear the steady rhythm of his heart.

"So," he said, breaking the comfortable silence, "we have some planning to do. I should return to Frostfjord soon. I left rather…abruptly."

"Abruptly?"

"Well… I left without telling anyone but my sister," I said with a laugh. "But I did leave a note behind."

"Oh, Bjorn," I said with a laugh.

"My family will be wondering about me, and I'll need to tell them about us."

"Do you think they'll approve?" I asked, unable to keep the worry from my voice. "Your mother…"

"My father will be surprised but ultimately supportive. He's always been more concerned with our happiness than political alliances." He hesitated. "My mother may take more convincing, but she'll come around once she meets you."

"And if she doesn't?"

"She will," he said firmly. "I know her. She will be as charmed by you as I am."

The conviction in his voice soothed my fears somewhat. "And what about after? Would I be expected to live in Frostfjord? What about The Sconery?"

"The life you've built here is beautiful. I would never ask you to leave it, but I would ask to be part of it."

"Would that be okay with your family?"

"I have four siblings. Plenty of royal heirs to go around. It will be all right. Although, we will probably have to visit occasionally, and you will have to learn our anthem."

"That song?"

Bjorn laughed. "Yes. That song. And I need to warn you, the royal attire is very uncomfortable."

"As long as I can cut some holes for my wings, I can make it work."

Bjorn kissed my head. "Thank you, Rosalyn. Thank you for your forgiveness…and for seeing *me*."

"Oh, Bjorn," I whispered. "There is nothing to forgive. You're everything I've ever dreamed of. I can't wait to start our life together."

And with that, we kissed again, visions of a golden future—part ice and snow, part sugar and flour—dancing through my mind.

EPILOGUE: ROSALYN
TWO MONTHS LATER...

The mirror reflected a bride I hardly recognized.

My wedding gown was a masterpiece of magical craftsmanship with layers of frost-white silk that shimmered with crystalline-like enchantments, catching the light like freshly fallen snow. Silver embroidery traced intricate patterns across the bodice, echoing the royal runes of Frostfjord while incorporating delicate flowers, butterflies, and other pixie symbolism. The long, flowing sleeves were edged with crystalized moon blossoms that would never wilt, and the train behind me seemed to float like morning mist. Most remarkable was the special design that accommodated my wings, framing them with delicate silver filigree that enhanced rather than concealed their natural beauty.

Merry sat regally on a velvet cushion nearby, his golden horn polished to a brilliant shine for the occasion. The caticorn had surprised everyone by adapting remarkably well to the journey through Kellen's hollow trees, magical passageways which allowed one to take far journeys without ever stepping on a boat. Merry emerged from the portal with a smug expression that said, "Of course I handled it perfectly. I'm Merry." Now, he wore a tiny silver collar adorned with miniature frost crystals that matched my gown, looking every bit the noble companion.

"You look absolutely enchanting," my mother, Rin, said, her voice soft as she adjusted my elaborate headdress, a pixie-style crown of blue ice roses and crystallized moon blossoms that Winifred had crafted for the occasion.

"Thank you, Mother," I replied, still surprised she had made the journey. When she'd initially hesitated, claiming the winter travel would be hard on her health, I'd resigned myself to her absence. When she arrived with the last group from Moonshine Hollow, transported through Kellen's hollow tree network, I felt surprisingly relieved.

"I wouldn't have missed this for anything," she'd told me, embracing me. "Even though I needed a few special elixirs for the ride through the trees," she said with a tinkling laugh. "My daughter is marrying a prince. I have to be here. But prince or not, as long as you are happy, Rosalyn, that's all that matters."

"Thank you, Mother."

She tilted her head, eyeing my makeup once more. "More glitter," she said, opening her makeup case and applying more glitter to the corners of my eyes."

"Kellen deserves a medal for getting everyone here safely," Primrose remarked, straightening the folds of her ice-blue bridesmaid dress. "Those hollow tree passages are not for the faint of heart."

"It was quite the experience," my mother agreed. "Like being wrapped in living bark and whisked through the earth itself. Efficient, if unsettling."

"I'm so grateful to him," I said.

From across the room, Zarina, my kitchen witch apprentice, approached. Her dark eyes shimmered with both excitement and slight awe at the grandeur of everything.

"You look beautiful, Rosalyn. Please enjoy your time here, and don't worry about anything at home. I'll see to The Sconery."

I gave her arm an affectionate squeeze. "I know it's in good hands with you."

"Speaking of home," Juniper interjected, adjusting her gown, "I'll need to head back shortly after the festivities. Granik's new crop is showing unusual magical properties, and he's completely baffled." A soft smile played across her lips as she mentioned the orc farmer. "You know how he gets when his plants do unexpected things."

I raised an eyebrow, noting the gentle blush that colored Juniper's cheeks at the mention of Granik.

"Best get back soon, then. He'll be lost without your expertise," I commented, exchanging a knowing glance with Primrose, who also noticed Juniper's rosy cheeks.

Primrose winked at me.

"Oh, he's quite capable," Juniper replied, her blush deepening. "He just…appreciates my perspective."

"I'm sure he does," Winifred muttered from where she

was smoothing the train of my dress, a knowing tone in her voice.

Primrose cleared her throat. Changing the subject, she said, "I hope you and Bjorn will return for the library's birthday celebration."

"We wouldn't miss it," I assured her. "I know it will be great."

"Good." Primrose nodded, then added under her breath, "If I can pull it off, that is."

"Is there a problem with the celebration planning?" I asked.

"What? Oh, no," Primrose said quickly—too quickly. "Just the usual planning challenges. Nothing for you to worry about on your wedding day."

Emmalyn peeked in before I could press further, her cheeks flushed with excitement. "It's time," she announced. "Everyone's assembled in the great hall."

My heart skipped a beat.

This was the moment Bjorn and I would officially join our lives together.

With Emmalyn, Primrose, Juniper, Zarina, and Winifred, who was carrying Merry, accompanying me, we made our way to the great hall. My friends were dressed in beautiful gowns of various shades of Frostfjord blue and held bouquets of blue roses.

My mother took my arm, guiding me.

"I am so proud of you, Rosalyn. I know we had a difference of opinion when you left Spring Haven, but you are an exceptional woman."

"Thank you, Mother," I whispered, kissing her cheek.

"Your lipstick," my mother chided.

"It's enchanted. No smearing."

My mother laughed.

Following an attendant, we made our way to the doors of the great hall.

On the other side, a horn sounded, and a harp announced the beginning of the ceremony with a triumphant glissando.

The huge wooden doors opened, revealing the crowd inside.

The massive pillars had been decorated in garlands of blue roses and greens. Overhead, chandeliers burned brightly. The hall's ceiling had been enchanted to look like the northern lights, ripples of purple and blue waving before a starry background. Snow fell softly, creating a pleasing ambiance but never reaching the assembly. A crowd of well-dressed northerners watched as we entered. Along with them were Tansy and Kellen and Elder Thornberry and Lady Petunia—whose nose was red from the cold.

The hall's beauty was nothing compared to the man waiting for me.

With his parents and siblings in attendance, Bjorn stepped forward, waiting for me. He stood tall and proud in the traditional formal wear of Frostfjord royalty: a deep blue tunic embroidered with silver runes, a short cloak lined with silk, and his royal silver torc gleaming at his throat. His hair had been pulled up in a bun, revealing his face's strong lines. Smoke sat faithfully at his side, the firewolf wearing a silver collar that complemented Bjorn's attire, his ember-flecked fur groomed to a lustrous shine. But it was Bjorn's expression that caught my heart. A look of absolute wonder and love was painted on his face as he watched me approach.

Behind him stood his family, including the king and queen and all Bjorn's siblings. Bjorn had been right. It had taken little effort to win over Queen Maren. The gracious queen had greeted me warmly, impressed that someone had finally won Bjorn's heart.

"Shall we?" my mother whispered.

I nodded.

Fluttering our wings, we made our way to the front of the hall, flying up to the dais rather than walking up the stairs.

When we met Bjorn, my mother set my hand in his.

Bjorn leaned forward, kissing Rin on her cheek, and then my mother stepped aside with my friends.

"You look so beautiful," Bjorn whispered, "like the Lady of Spring herself."

"You're not so bad yourself," I replied with a wink. "And you definitely need to fix your hair like that more often."

Bjorn chuckled.

With that, we turned our attention to the officiants.

The ceremony itself was a blend of traditions, with Rune elf formality and touches of pixie custom woven throughout. We exchanged vows, bound our hands with a silver cord embedded with northern and southern magic, and shared the traditional blessing cup of wine.

"Prince Bjorn, what gift do you offer your bride as a token of your love?" the officiant asked.

"An arm ring forged here in the Frozen Isles," Bjorn said, slipping the ringlet of silver up my arm to my bicep. "It is made from the first neck torc I was granted as a boy. May it symbolize my lifelong love."

"Rosalyn, what gift do you offer your husband as a token of your love?"

I grinned at Bjorn, then pulled a small, folded piece of paper from my sleeve. "I considered giving you a ring or an amulet, but nothing felt quite right. I wanted to give you something that showed my undying trust." I grinned. "So, I gift this to you, Bjorn, the recipe for my rose-and-strawberry scones, an award-winning and absolutely secret recipe known only to me… and now to you. You are the only man I have ever dreamed of sharing my life with, and to prove it, I give you my most coveted secret."

At that, the crowd laughed.

Bjorn chuckled. "Your secrets and scones are safe with me."

I smiled warmly at him.

"Prince Bjorn of Frostfjord," the officiant called, "and Rosalyn Hartwood of Moonshine Hollow, hailing from the pixie lands of Spring Haven, I confirm that your tokens have been exchanged and your vows completed. Therefore, before this good audience, I am pleased to pronounce you husband and wife! Kiss the one you love, and let us all revel in your joy."

With that, Bjorn leaned forward and set a passionate kiss on my lips.

The crowd erupted in cheers, sparks flying all around the room from the traditional pixie wands my mother had brought from Spring Haven. Colorful, magical confetti popped alongside golden sparks, lighting the great hall with color and light.

The musicians began to play, and the whole room broke out in smiles and excited cheers.

King Ramr and Queen Maren stepped forward to congratulate us.

"Well done," Queen Maren said as she embraced me, her formal façade softening slightly. "Welcome to the family, Rosalyn."

"Thank you, Your Majesty," I replied, still a bit nervous around my new mother-in-law despite her kindness.

"Maren, please," she corrected gently. "We are family now."

King Ramr, overcome with joy, pulled my tiny mother into an embrace. "Oh, aye. A pixie in our family now! Welcome, dear lady! Welcome."

"Oh!" my mother exclaimed in surprise. "Thank you. Thank you very much."

When he finally let her go, he turned to me, enfolding me in a bear hug that lifted me off the ground. "About time that boy found someone with spirit," he declared, his voice booming in the hall. "You'll bring some much-needed warmth to Frostfjord, my dear."

"Thank you, King Ramr."

Moments later, the great hall transformed. Servants quickly rearranged the space, using magic to bring in tables and heaps of food. Ice sculptures melted into colorful drinks while musicians played jaunty melodies.

The following celebration was joyful and loud, with all the local people joining the festivities.

I found myself drawn into conversation with Asa, who was holding her pearl-white caticorn kitten.

"Rosalyn," she said, "thank you again for sending me the kitten. I'm so grateful. He's so cute."

I scratched the kitten on the head. "And a fair bit friendlier than Merry," I said with a laugh. "I'm glad you like him."

Bjorn joined us. "Promise kept," he told his sister with a grin, petting the kitten.

"It was the least you could do since I aided and abetted your escape."

Bjorn chuckled then turned to me. "Speaking of, come with me," he said, taking my hand. "I want to show you something."

"You do know everyone wants to talk to you, right?" Asa needled her brother.

"Why do you think we're leaving?"

"Coward."

Chuckling, Bjorn pulled me away.

I waved goodbye to Asa and followed Bjorn as he led me away from the great hall, through a series of corridors, and up a winding staircase. We emerged onto a secluded balcony high on the palace's northern face, overlooking the frozen expanse of the village, port, and sea.

The view was breathtaking. The full moon cast a silvery glow over the ice-covered landscape, making it sparkle like a field of diamonds. In the distance, icebergs drifted slowly in the current, their shapes fantastical in the moonlight.

But what truly took my breath away was the sky above. From here, we could see the real northern lights. Ribbons of green, blue, and purple danced across the stars, shifting and swirling in patterns too beautiful to describe.

"The northern lights," Bjorn explained, standing behind me, his arms wrapping around my waist.

"They're magnificent," I breathed, unable to take my eyes off the spectacle. I leaned against him, savoring his warmth in the cold night air. After a moment, I carefully unfurled my wings, allowing them to catch the aurora's light. The magical dust that naturally shed from them shimmered in response to the northern lights, creating a miniature version of the celestial display around us.

"Beautiful, just like you," Bjorn whispered. "My wife..."

"My husband." I turned in his arms to face him, reaching up to trace one of the runes on his collarbone. It began to glow at my touch, the blue light spreading to the others until they formed a pattern of luminescence across his skin.

Bjorn leaned down to kiss me. The kiss was gentle at first, then deeper as he pulled me closer. When we finally broke apart, both a little breathless, I rested my head against his chest, listening to the steady rhythm of his heart.

"Are you happy?" he asked, his voice soft.

I thought about everything that had brought us to this moment—the serendipity of his arrival in Moonshine

Hollow, our connection over the unicorns, the magical working that had brought us closer, the misunderstandings and revelations, all the baking, and finally, the choice we'd both made to build a life together.

"More than I ever thought possible," I told him honestly.

Above us, the northern lights continued their dance.

As we stood there, wrapped in each other's arms with the beauty of Frostfjord spread before us and the promise of a life in Moonshine Hollow waiting for our return, I knew with absolute certainty that whatever adventures lay ahead, we would face them together. The baker and the prince, finding our own happily ever after.

ACKNOWLEDGEMENTS

With special thanks to Becky Stephens and Lindsay Galloway for their work on this series.

Thank you to all the readers in The Cozy Coven! Thank you for your hard work.

Thank you to the amazing people who are part of my readers' group, Maisy's Daisies! Thank you, Daisies!

ACKNOWLEDGEMENTS

Thank you to my family for their support on this new adventure.

Many thanks to Tee, Lila, Jillian, Laura, Olivia, Ariana, Heloise, Lucy, KD, and Emberlyn for being amazing author besties.

A Special Thank You to My Paid Patreons!
Y R
Tiffany S.
Dee F.
Becky
Megan
Deanna B.
Jesikah S.

ABOUT THE AUTHOR

Maisy Magill writes cozy fantasy romances where magic meets small-town charm—think *Stars Hollow* with a sprinkle of fairy dust and a pinch of spice to make things interesting. Her stories are the bookish equivalent of a warm hug, a crackling fire, and a perfectly baked scone (preferably with a touch of enchantment).

When she's not weaving tales of love, magic, and mischievous caticorns, Maisy fully embraces the cottagecore lifestyle. She can usually be found coaxing her garden into behaving, embroidering slightly wonky flowers, making chocolate or gelato (because why choose?), or sipping tea while pretending she'll only read *one more chapter*. Her books invite readers to slow down, savor the magic, and believe in love, one whimsical, heartwarming story at a time.

Connect with Maisy Online
MaisyMagill.com

RECIPES FROM MOONSHINE HOLLOW

Dear Cozy Friend,

I'm so glad you've wandered into my cozy corner of the internet. As a special gift to you, please enjoy these recipes inspired by the pages of Must Love Scones and Secrets. I hope each one brings a bit of magic to your day.

ROSALYN'S SECRET RECIPE: ROSE-AND-STRAWBERRY SCONES

These enchanting scones combine fresh strawberries with the delicate floral notes of rose, creating a treat as magical as Rosalyn Hartwood's touch in The Sconery.

This is Rosalyn's secret recipe, so keep it safe!

Ingredients:

- 2½ cups all-purpose flour
- ⅓ cup granulated sugar
- 2½ teaspoons baking powder
- ½ teaspoon salt
- ½ cup unsalted butter, chilled and cubed
- ¾ cup heavy cream
- 1 large egg
- 1 teaspoon vanilla extract
- 1 teaspoon rose extract
- 1 cup fresh strawberries, diced
- 2 tablespoons edible rose petals (plus extra for garnish)

For the glaze:

- 1 cup powdered sugar
- 2–3 tablespoons milk
- ¼ teaspoon rose extract

Instructions:

1. Preheat your oven to 400°F (200°C). Line a baking sheet with parchment paper.
2. In a large bowl, whisk together the flour, sugar, baking powder, and salt.
3. Add the cubed butter and cut it into the flour mixture using a pastry cutter or your fingers until it resembles coarse crumbs.
4. In a separate bowl, whisk together the heavy cream, egg, vanilla extract, and rose extract.
5. Pour the wet ingredients into the dry mixture and stir until just combined. Be careful not to overmix.
6. Gently fold in the diced strawberries and rose petals. The dough will be slightly sticky.
7. Turn the dough out onto a lightly floured surface and shape it into a 1-inch-thick circle.
8. Cut the dough into 8 wedges and place them on the prepared baking sheet.
9. Bake for 15–18 minutes or until the scones are golden brown. Remove from the oven and let cool slightly on a wire rack.
10. While the scones are cooling, make the glaze by whisking together the powdered sugar, milk, and rose extract until smooth. Adjust the consistency with more milk or powdered sugar as needed.
11. Drizzle the glaze over the scones, then garnish

with additional edible rose petals for a magical touch.
12. Serve warm or at room temperature with a cup of floral tea, like jasmine or chamomile, for a truly enchanting experience.

ROSALYN'S FORGET ME SCONES (BLUEBERRY & CHAMOMILE)

Ingredients:

- 2 cups all-purpose flour
- ⅓ cup granulated sugar
- 1 tablespoon baking powder
- ½ teaspoon salt
- 2 tablespoons culinary-grade dried chamomile flowers
- 8 tablespoons (1 stick) cold unsalted butter, cubed
- 1 cup fresh blueberries
- ½ cup heavy cream, plus more for brushing
- 1 large egg
- 2 teaspoons vanilla extract
- 2 tablespoons blue butterfly pea flower powder (for color) or blue food coloring (optional)
- Coarse sugar for sprinkling (optional)

Instructions:

1. Preheat your oven to 400°F (200°C). Line a baking sheet with parchment paper.
2. In a large bowl, whisk together the flour, sugar, baking powder, salt, and chamomile flowers.
3. Add the cold cubed butter to the flour mixture. Using a pastry cutter or your fingertips, work the butter into the flour until it resembles coarse crumbs with some pea-sized pieces remaining.
4. Gently fold in the blueberries, being careful not to crush them.
5. In a separate bowl, whisk together the heavy cream, egg, vanilla extract, and blue butterfly pea flower powder or food coloring.
6. Pour the wet ingredients over the dry ingredients and stir gently with a fork until just combined. The dough will be shaggy and somewhat sticky.
7. Turn the dough out onto a lightly floured surface and gently knead a few times until it comes together. Pat into a circle about 1-inch thick.
8. Cut the circle into 8 wedges and transfer to the prepared baking sheet, leaving about 2 inches between each scone.
9. Brush the tops with additional heavy cream and sprinkle with coarse sugar if desired.
10. Bake for 18–22 minutes, or until the scones are golden brown with a hint of blue and a

toothpick inserted into the center comes out clean.
11. Allow to cool on the baking sheet for 5 minutes before transferring to a wire rack.
12. For maximum enchantment, serve warm with a cup of chamomile tea while contemplating happier days ahead.

ROSALYN'S CROWD PLEASER SCONES (ORANGE & HONEY)

Ingredients:

- 2 cups all-purpose flour
- ¼ cup granulated sugar
- 1 tablespoon baking powder
- ½ teaspoon salt
- ¼ teaspoon baking soda
- Zest of 2 medium oranges
- 8 tablespoons (1 stick) cold unsalted butter, cubed
- ½ cup buttermilk
- 1 large egg
- ¼ cup honey, plus more for glaze
- 1 teaspoon vanilla extract

For the glaze:

- 1 cup powdered sugar
- 2 tablespoons fresh orange juice
- 1 tablespoon honey
- ½ teaspoon orange zest

Instructions:

1. Preheat oven to 400°F (200°C). Line a baking sheet with parchment paper.
2. In a large bowl, whisk together the flour, sugar, baking powder, salt, baking soda, and orange zest.
3. Add the cold cubed butter to the flour mixture. Using a pastry cutter or your fingertips, work the butter into the flour until it resembles coarse crumbs with some pea-sized pieces remaining.
4. In a separate bowl, whisk together the buttermilk, egg, honey, and vanilla extract until well combined.
5. Pour the wet ingredients over the dry ingredients and stir gently with a fork until just combined. Be careful not to overmix.
6. Turn the dough out onto a lightly floured surface and gently knead a few times until it comes together. Pat into a circle about 1-inch thick.
7. Cut the circle into 8 wedges and transfer to the prepared baking sheet, leaving about 2 inches between each scone.

8. Bake for 15–18 minutes, or until the scones are golden brown and a toothpick inserted into the center comes out clean.
9. While the scones are baking, prepare the glaze by whisking together the powdered sugar, orange juice, honey, and orange zest until smooth.
10. Allow the scones to cool for 5 minutes on the baking sheet, then transfer to a wire rack placed over a piece of parchment paper (to catch drips).
11. While the scones are still warm, drizzle the glaze over the top, allowing it to run down the sides.
12. For maximum cheer, serve warm with a cup of your favorite tea and watch as smiles appear with each bite.

THE MOONLIT CHALICE'S BLOOMBERRY* TARTS

Ingredients:

For the Tart Shells:

- 1½ cups all-purpose flour
- ½ cup powdered sugar
- ¼ teaspoon salt
- ½ cup (1 stick) cold unsalted butter, cubed
- 1 large egg yolk

- 2 tablespoons ice water
- 1 teaspoon vanilla extract

For the Creamy Filling:

- 8 ounces cream cheese, softened
- ⅓ cup granulated sugar
- 1 teaspoon vanilla extract
- 1 tablespoon lemon zest
- 2 tablespoons heavy cream

For the Bloomberry Topping:

- 3 cups fresh bloomberries*
- ½ cup granulated sugar
- 2 tablespoons cornstarch
- 2 tablespoons lemon juice
- ¼ cup water
- 1 tablespoon butter

*Note: Since bloomberries are exclusive to Moonshine Hollow and unavailable in our world, fresh raspberries make an excellent substitute. Their bright flavor and vibrant color perfectly mimic the magical bloomberries from Elder Thornberry's vineyard. For an extra magical touch, you can add a drop of pink food coloring to enhance the distinctive bloomberry glow!

Instructions:

1. Prepare the tart shells: In a food processor, pulse together flour, powdered sugar, and salt. Add cold butter cubes and pulse until the mixture resembles coarse crumbs. Add egg yolk, ice water, and vanilla, then pulse just until dough comes together.
2. Press the dough into 6 individual 4-inch tart pans with removable bottoms (or one 9-inch tart pan). Prick the bottoms with a fork. Refrigerate for 30 minutes.
3. Preheat oven to 375°F (190°C). Line the chilled tart shells with parchment paper and fill with pie weights or dried beans. Bake for 15 minutes, then remove weights and parchment and bake for another 5–10 minutes until golden. Cool completely.
4. Make the creamy filling: Beat cream cheese, sugar, vanilla, and lemon zest until smooth and fluffy. Add heavy cream and beat until well incorporated. Refrigerate until ready to use.
5. Prepare the bloomberry topping: In a saucepan, combine 2 cups of raspberries, sugar, cornstarch, lemon juice, and water. Bring to a simmer over medium heat, stirring frequently until thickened, about 5–7 minutes. Remove from heat and stir in butter. Let cool completely.
6. Assemble the tarts: Spread the cream cheese filling evenly into cooled tart shells. Top with the cooked bloomberry mixture, then arrange the

remaining fresh raspberries on top in a decorative pattern.
7. Refrigerate the tarts for at least 2 hours before serving to allow the filling to set properly.
8. For an extra touch of Moonshine Hollow magic, dust with a little edible shimmer before serving to mimic the famous glow of bloomberries in the moonlight.

ROSALYN'S FARMER'S PIE

Ingredients

For the filling:

- 1 tablespoon olive oil or butter
- 1 small onion, chopped
- 2 cloves garlic, minced
- 2 cups frozen mixed vegetables (like peas, carrots, corn, and green beans)
- 1 (15 oz) can lentils, drained and rinsed *(or 1½ cups cooked brown lentils)*
- 1 tablespoon tomato paste
- ½ cup vegetable broth or water
- 1 teaspoon dried thyme
- ½ teaspoon smoked paprika (optional)
- Salt and pepper, to taste

RECIPES FROM MOONSHINE HOLLOW

For the topping:

- 2 cups instant mashed potatoes, prepared according to package instructions
- 2 tablespoons butter or plant-based butter
- ¼ cup milk or non-dairy milk
- Salt and pepper to taste
- Optional: ½ cup shredded cheddar or plant-based cheese

Instructions

1. Preheat oven to 375°F (190°C).
2. Make the filling: In a large skillet, heat olive oil over medium heat. Sauté onion until soft, about 4–5 minutes. Add garlic and cook for 1 minute more. Stir in frozen vegetables, lentils, tomato paste, broth, thyme, paprika, salt, and pepper. Simmer for 5–7 minutes until warmed through and slightly thickened. Spread the mixture evenly in a greased 8x8" baking dish.
3. Prepare the mashed potatoes: Make the mashed potatoes according to the package, adding butter and milk until creamy. Season with salt and pepper.
4. Assemble: Spoon mashed potatoes over the vegetable filling. Use the back of a spoon or fork to spread evenly and create decorative ridges. Sprinkle cheese over the top if using.

5. Bake for 20–25 minutes or until golden and bubbly. Broil for the last 2–3 minutes for a browned top, if desired.
6. Cool slightly and serve warm.

ROSALYN'S CREAMY BUTTERNUT SQUASH SOUP

Ingredients

- 2 tablespoons unsalted butter
- 1 tablespoon olive oil
- 1 medium onion, diced
- 2 cloves garlic, minced
- 1 (20–24 oz) bag frozen butternut squash
- 4 cups vegetable broth
- ½ teaspoon ground nutmeg
- Salt and freshly ground black pepper to taste
- ½ cup heavy whipping cream

Instructions

1. Sauté Aromatics: In a large pot, melt the butter and olive oil over medium heat. Add diced onion and cook until soft, about 5–7 minutes. Add the garlic and cook for 1 more minute.

2. Simmer the Squash: Add the frozen butternut squash and vegetable broth. Bring to a boil, then reduce heat and simmer for 15–20 minutes until the squash is completely tender.
3. Blend Smooth: Use an immersion blender (or regular blender in batches) to puree the soup until smooth and creamy.
4. Add Cream & Seasoning: Stir in the nutmeg, salt, and pepper. Add the heavy cream and warm through gently for 5 more minutes—do not boil.
5. Serve Warm: Ladle into bowls and enjoy with warm bread or a scone on the side.

THE SURLY DRAGON'S LEMON SMASH COCKTAIL

Ingredients

- 2 oz gin (botanical gin works best)
- ½ cup cold lemonade (store-bought or homemade)
- 4–5 fresh mint leaves (fresh basil also works)
- Ice
- Lemon slice and mint sprig for garnish

Instructions

1. In a cocktail shaker or sturdy glass, gently muddle the mint leaves to release their aroma— a light press, not a full crush.
2. Add the gin and lemonade. Fill with ice and shake or stir briskly until well chilled.
3. Strain into a glass filled with ice.
4. Add a lemon slice and a mint sprig for a bright, inviting finish.

I hope these recipes brought a little Moonshine Hollow magic into your kitchen.

If you enjoyed this taste of Moonshine Hollow and want more recipes, behind-the-scenes sneak peeks, and exclusive extras, I'd love to welcome you to my Patreon for more enchanted goodies.

Find out more at patreon.com/maisymagill

Warm wishes,
Maisy